THE GREAT GATSBY

SILVER EDITION

F. SCOTT FITZGERALD

EDITED BY
ADAPTIVE READER

ISBN: 979-8-8693-0814-6

INTRODUCTION

Welcome to Adaptive Reader, your portal to the captivating world of literature, tailored to fit your unique reading abilities.

In today's fast-paced and diverse learning environment, we believe in the power of personalized learning experiences. That's where the concept of leveled reading comes in, and why we, at Adaptive Reader, have dedicated ourselves to offering a broad collection of classic novels at various reading levels. Our mission is to make the joy and benefits of reading accessible to everyone.

THE BENEFITS OF LEVELED TEXTS

So, what exactly is leveled reading? It's an approach that matches students with texts that align with their unique reading abilities. This ensures that every reader is challenged just the right amount - enough to grow, but not so much that they feel overwhelmed or frustrated.

For students, this means you'll engage with texts that stretch your reading skills while keeping the experience enjoyable and manageable. You'll gain confidence as you successfully comprehend each level and feel motivated to explore more challenging texts as your reading skills grow.

For teachers, Adaptive Reader provides a valuable tool to support differentiated instruction. You can assign the same novel to your entire class while ensuring each student reads a version that aligns with their reading level. This allows all students to participate in class discussions and activities, fostering a more inclusive learning environment.

For parents, Adaptive Reader offers a supportive tool to encourage your children's reading journey. As your child progresses through the different levels of a novel, they'll not only enhance their reading skills but also develop a deeper love for literature.

READING ACROSS MULTIPLE EDITIONS

All of our leveled novels include passage markers that correspond to the same content across every one of our editions. This means that passage '62' in our silver edition contains the same themes and plot elements as passage '62' in our original edition.

For teachers, this means that you can say "let's look at passage 35 together. What is the author trying to tell us here?" and all of your students will be reading the same content — but with vocabulary and syntax that's adapted to their reading level.

Our online reading tool, available at www.adaptivereader.com, gives students and teachers free access to the original text with passage markers. We encourage teachers to include close readings of the original text as part of their coursework, giving all students exposure to the rich original syntax and language of these exceptional authors.

THE POWER OF LITERATURE

At Adaptive Reader, we are committed to helping everyone experience the power of literature. So whether you're a student diving into a classic novel, a teacher looking for flexible resources, or a parent seeking ways to support your child's literacy, Adaptive Reader is here for you.

We invite you to embark on this exciting literary journey with us. Enjoy the world of stories, characters, and ideas that await you in our collection of leveled novels. Happy reading!

CHAPTER

ONE

WHEN I WAS YOUNGER, my dad told me something that I think about a lot. He said, "Before you say something bad about someone, remember that not everyone has had the same chances as you."

He didn't say anything more, but I knew he meant a lot more than that. As a result, I've learned to not judge people right away. It's a habit that has helped me get to know many interesting people, but it has also made me listen to a lot of boring stories. When someone seems different from everybody else, it's easy for me to notice and get to know them. This is why people in college thought I was a politician, because I knew the secrets of others. Most of the time, these people would share their secrets without me even asking. Sometimes, I would pretend to be asleep or too busy to listen when I knew someone was about to tell me something personal. Young men often share their feelings in ways that they've heard before, and they don't always tell the whole story. Not judging others gives me hope. I'm still a little scared that I might forget that some people are taught to be kinder than others.

I have my limits when it comes to getting to know others, though. People's actions can be based on good or bad intentions, but there's a point where I stop caring about their reasons. When I came back from the East last year, for example, I wished the world would be more polite and proper. I didn't want any more wild adventures or glimpses into people's hearts.

However, there was one person who I found interesting—the man named Gatsby, who this book is all about. I had a strong dislike for everything he stood for, but he had this special quality that made him interesting. It was like he could sense the excitement of life even from far away, like someone who could feel an earthquake about to shake the earth's surface. He was a kind of dreamer, but not in a bad way. It was an incredible ability to have hope and be ready for romantic experiences, something I haven't seen in anyone else and probably won't see again. No, Gatsby ended up being okay in the end. It's what haunted him and the destruction caused by his dreams that made me lose interest in the ups and downs of other people's lives.

My family has been well-known and successful in this midwestern city for three generations. The Carraways believe we're descended from the Dukes of Buccleuch. However, the real founder of our family was my grandfather's brother. He came here in 1851, didn't fight in the Civil War because he sent someone else in his place, and started a wholesale hardware store that my father still runs today.

I never met this great-uncle, but I'm told that I look like him. There's a painting of him that hangs in my father's office, and it kind of looks like me.

In 1915, I graduated from New Haven University, 25 years after my father did. After that, I fought in World War I against the Germans. I enjoyed being a soldier in battle, so when I returned, I felt bored. Instead of feeling like the important center of the world, the middle of the country now seemed like the distant edge of every-thing to me. So, I made up my mind to go to the East and learn about the bond business.

It seemed like everyone I knew was already in that business, so I thought maybe it could support one more single man. My aunts and uncles all talked about it as if they were choosing a school for me, and eventually they said, "Yes, go ahead," but they seemed unsure and worried. My father agreed to provide money for me for a year and I came to the East for good in the spring of 1922.

In the warm season, I needed to find a place to live in the city. A man at work suggested that we rent a house in a town nearby. It seemed like a great idea, so we found a worn-out house for $80 a month. But then, my coworker had to go to Washington, so I ended up going to the town alone. I had a dog, but he ran away after a few days. I also had an old car and a Finnish cleaning lady who cooked for me and said wise things.

I felt lonely at first, but one morning a man, who was new in town, asked me for directions. I helped him and suddenly, I didn't feel lonely anymore. I felt like a guide, someone who knows the area and can help others. It was the start of summer, with the sunshine and the trees growing leaves. And just like in the movies, I felt like life was starting fresh again.

First of all, there were so many books to read, and the fresh, clean air made me feel healthy. I bought twelve books about money and business. They looked fancy on my bookshelf, like new coins, promising to reveal secrets about how to get rich. I planned to read many other books too. In college, I liked to write serious articles for the school newspaper. Now, I wanted to bring that learning back into my life and become a person who knows a little bit about every-thing. However, life is actually easier when you focus on just one thing at a time.

I was lucky to find a house in one of the strangest places in North America. This place is located on a long, chaotic island that is east from New York. There are some unusual land formations there. Twenty miles from the city, there are two giant, identical egg-shaped peninsulas that are only separated by a small bay. They stick out into the very calm saltwater of Long Island Sound. The eggs are not perfect ovals, they are flat on one end, like when an egg gets squished. It must be amazing for the seagulls flying above to see such similar shapes. But what's even more interesting is that, other than the shape and size, these eggs are completely different.

I lived in West Egg, which was less fancy than the other one nearby. But this doesn't really show how strange and even a little scary the contrast between them was. My house was at the very end of West Egg, only fifty yards from the Sound. It was squeezed between two huge places that people rented for a lot of money during the summer. The one on my right was really big and fancy. It looked like a big house in France, with a tower on one side. It was still very new and had ivy growing on it. There was even a fancy swimming pool made of marble, and the property was over forty acres with a big lawn and garden. That was where a rich man named Gatsby lived, or at least that's what people said. Now, my house wasn't as nice. It was kind of ugly, but it was small and no one really noticed it. I had a view of the water and could see part of my neighbor's lawn. Plus, there were a lot of rich people around, which made me feel a little better about where I lived. And the best part was, I only paid eighty dollars a month for it.

On the other side of the bay, there were fancy white houses of East Egg that sparkled along the water. The story of that summer really starts when I went over there for dinner at the Tom Buchanans' house. Daisy, who was my cousin, and I had known Tom back in college. And just after the war, I had spent a couple of days with them in Chicago.

Her husband was really good at football when he was in college, and even today he's known for being one of the best. He was so good at just twenty-one years old that everything he did after that seemed like a letdown. His family had a ton of money—people used to criticize him for spending too much in college. But now he had left Chicago and moved to the East Coast in such an unbelievable rich guy way. For example, he brought a whole bunch of polo horses with him from Lake Forest. I couldn't believe that someone my age could be so rich.

I'm not sure why they moved to the East Coast. They had spent a year in France for no real reason, and then just went to wherever rich people played polo. Daisy said it was a permanent move when we talked on the phone, but I didn't believe her. I never really understood Daisy's feelings, but I felt like Tom would always be searching for the excitement and drama of his football days.

One warm, windy evening, I drove to East Egg to visit my cousin and her husband. They were like two old friends whom I barely knew. Their house was fancier than I imagined, a big red-and-white mansion with a view of the bay. The lawn stretched from the beach to the front door, full of sundials, brick paths, and beautiful gardens. It even climbed up the side of the house with vines, as if it couldn't stop running. There were big windows at the front of the house, glowing with gold light and open to the warm afternoon breeze. Tom Buchanan was standing on the front porch, wearing riding clothes and looking confident.

He looked different from his college days at New Haven. Now he was a strong-looking man with straw-colored hair and a bit of a mean expression. His eyes were bright and confident, and he seemed like he was always leaning forward aggressively. Even though his riding clothes had a fancy style, you could tell he had a very muscular body. It seemed like his muscles were so big that they were straining against his boots, and you could see his muscles moving when he moved his shoulders. He had a powerful body.

His voice sounded rough and low, like a deep singing voice. It made him seem like a stubborn, grumpy person. Even when he liked someone, there was a little bit of disrespect in his voice, as if he thought he was stronger and more important than them. Some guys at college really hated him, even though we were in the same class. We weren't close, but I always felt like he wanted me to like him. It always made me a little uneasy.

We chatted for a little while on the sunny porch.

"I have a nice house here," he said, his eyes quickly looking around.

He put his hand flat on my arm and turned me to look at the front view. His hand swept across a sunken Italian garden, a big field of sweet-smelling roses, and a short motorboat that bobbed in the water.

"This used to belong to a guy named Demaine, who worked in the oil business." He turned me around again, politely but suddenly. "Let's go inside."

We walked into a pretty room with big windows on each end. The windows were open and the sunlight made the room glow. The breeze blew, making the curtains flutter and swing in the wind. The only thing that wasn't moving was a huge couch where two young women sat. They were wearing white dresses that looked like they were floating, as if they had just come inside after flying around. I stood there for a moment. Then Tom Buchanan closed the windows, and everything became still. The curtains fell to the floor and the young women stopped looking like they were floating.

The younger girl was someone I didn't know. She was lying down on the couch, not moving at all. Her chin was slightly lifted, like she was trying to balance something on it. If she noticed me, she didn't show it. I felt like I should apologize for bothering her.

The other girl, Daisy, tried to stand up. She leaned forward and had a serious look on her face. Then she laughed, a cute and silly laugh. I laughed too and walked into the room.

"I'm so happy to see you!"

She laughed again, like she said something very clever. She held my hand and looked up at me, telling me that there was no one else she wanted to see. That's how she was. She quietly told me that the other girl's last name was Baker. (Some people said that Daisy only whispered to make people pay more attention to her. It didn't matter, she was still charming.)

Either way, Miss Baker's lips moved slightly. She nodded at me. Again, I felt like I was annoying her. However, I'm always impressed by people who seem like they don't need anyone else.

I looked at my cousin, who started asking me questions in her soft, exciting voice. Her voice made me want to follow every word, like they were notes in a song that I would never hear again. Her voice had a way of making men who cared for her feel special. She was unforgettable. She whispered "Listen," as if she had just experienced something thrilling and there were more exciting things to come.

I told her how I had taken a break in Chicago and how people had sent their love to her through me.

"Do they miss me?" she asked with excitement.

"The whole town feels empty without you. All the cars have their left rear wheel painted black to show their sadness. There's a constant crying sound along the north shore at night."

"How amazing! Let's go back, Tom. Tomorrow!" Then she added, not really related to the conversation, "You should see the baby."

"I would love to."

"She's sleeping. She's three years old. Have you never seen her?"

"Never."

"Well, you should see her. She's—"

Tom Buchanan, who had been wandering around the room, came over and put his hand on my shoulder.

"What do you do, Nick?"

"I work with bonds."

"Who for?"

I told him.

"I've never heard of them," he stated firmly.

That annoyed me.

"You will," I replied shortly. "You will if you stay in the East."

"Oh, I'm staying in the East for sure," he said confidently, looking at Daisy and then back at me. It seemed like he was expecting something else. Miss Baker suddenly spoke up, saying "Absolutely!" with a suddenness that surprised both me and her. She yawned and stood up, complaining that she had been lying on the sofa for a long time.

"Don't blame me," Daisy responded, "I've been trying to get you to New York all afternoon."

"No, thanks," Miss Baker didn't want the cocktails that had been offered. "I'm training and can't have them."

Her host looked at her in disbelief. "You are! I don't know how you get anything done."

I looked at Miss Baker, wondering what she does. She was a slender girl with a straight posture, like a young soldier. Her gray eyes looked back at me with a polite curiosity from her face. It suddenly struck me that I had seen her somewhere before, or maybe a picture of her.

"You live in West Egg," she said with contempt. "I know someone there."

"I don't know anyone—"

"You must know Gatsby."

16

"Who's Gatsby?" asked Daisy curiously.

Before I could respond that he was my neighbor, dinner was announced. Tom Buchanan dragged me out of the room like a man moving a checker on a board.

Gracefully, with their hands on their hips, the two young women walked ahead of us to a porch bathed in rosy light, facing the sunset. There were candles on the table.

"Why are there candles?" Daisy asked, frowning. She quickly put them out with her fingers. "It's still light out and soon it'll be the longest day of the year." She looked at all of us with joy. "Do you always look forward to the longest day of the year and then miss it? I do."

"We should plan something," Miss Baker yawned, sitting down at the table as if getting into bed.

"Okay," Daisy said. "What should we plan?" She turned to me for help. "What do people usually plan?"

Before I could answer, her eyes focused on her little finger with an expression of awe.

"Look!" she exclaimed. "It hurts."

We all looked at her hand. The knuckle was black and blue.

"You did it, Tom," she accused. "I know you didn't mean to, but you did it. That's what I get for marrying a rough man, a big, strong, physically imposing—"

"I dislike the word 'imposing'," interrupted Tom irritably, "even as a joke."

"Imposing," Daisy insisted.

Sometimes Daisy and Miss Baker talked together, casually and with a playful lightness that wasn't quite chattering. They were cool like their white dresses and seemed uninterested in anything else.

"Daisy, you make me feel uncivilized," I admitted after my second glass of not-so-good wine. "Can't we talk about something ordinary, like crops?"

I didn't mean anything specific by my comment, but it sparked an unexpected response.

"Civilization is falling apart," Tom burst out angrily. "I've become a terrible pessimist. I've been reading a book about how the white race will be completely overwhelmed. It's all based on science. It's been proven."

"No, I haven't," I replied, surprised by his statement.

"Tom's become very serious," Daisy said sadly, her expression showing she hadn't really thought about it. "He reads complicated books with long words. What was that word we..."

"We all have to be careful," Tom said earnestly. "These books are about science and we need to pay attention, or other races might become more powerful than us."

Daisy nodded and whispered, "We have to stay on top." She blinked at me as if sharing a secret.

"You should live in California," Miss Baker started to say, but Tom interrupted her by shifting in his seat.

"The idea is that we, the Nordics, are responsible for all the things that make civilization great—like science and art," Tom explained.

He seemed so focused, as if his confidence wasn't enough anymore. Just then, the phone rang and the butler left the room. Daisy quickly leaned towards me.

"I have a secret to tell you," she whispered excitedly. "It's about the butler's nose. Do you want to hear?"

"That's the whole reason why I came tonight," I joked.

"Well, he used to polish silver for people in New York. He did it all day long, and it started to affect his nose..."

"Things got worse and worse," Miss Baker added.

"Yes, things got worse and worse until he had to quit his job."

The last bit of sunlight shone on her face and made it look beautiful. Her voice captivated me as I listened.

The butler returned and said something quietly to Tom. Tom looked upset, pushed his chair back, and went inside without saying anything.

Daisy said, "I love having you at my table, Nick. You remind me of a...a beautiful rose. Don't you?" She looked at Miss Baker for agreement. "A lovely rose?"

That wasn't true. I don't look anything like a rose. She was just making it up, but her words made me feel special.

Miss Baker and I exchanged a quick look without saying anything. Just as I was about to speak, Miss Baker sat up and said "Shh!" in a warning voice. We could hear quiet, passionate voices from the room next to us. Miss Baker leaned forward, trying to listen. The voices started to make sense, then stopped completely.

"This man Mr. Gatsby you mentioned is my neighbor," I started.

"Shh! I want to hear what's happening."

"Is something going on?" I asked innocently.

"You mean you don't know? Why..." she hesitated. "Tom has another woman in New York."

"Another woman?" I repeated, not understanding.

Miss Baker nodded.

"She should at least have the decency not to call him during dinner. Don't you think?"

Before I could fully understand, Tom and Daisy returned to the table.

"It couldn't be helped!" Daisy exclaimed with a forced cheerfulness.

She sat down, looked at Miss Baker and then at me, and continued, "I stepped outside for a moment, and it's so romantic out there. There's a bird on the lawn that I believe must be a nightingale that came on a ship. It's singing away…" Her voice sang: "It's romantic, right Tom?"

"Very romantic," he replied, and then sadly to me, "If it's still light outside after dinner, I want to show you the stables."

The telephone rang loudly inside the house, and Daisy shook her head at Tom to stop talking about the stables. Everything that was being discussed disappeared from our conversation. I also didn't want to look anyone in the eyes. I felt uncomfortable. I didn't know what Daisy and Tom were thinking, but even Miss Baker seemed unable to ignore the urgent and loud voice of the telephone, or "fifth guest."

Of course, we didn't talk about the horses again. Tom and Miss Baker walked back into the library, with some distance between them. It looked like they were keeping watch over something important. Daisy and I sat on the porch. She put her hand to her face and she seemed like she had a lot of strong feelings inside her. I asked her some comforting questions about her little girl.

"Nick, we don't really know each other well," she suddenly said. "Even though we're related. You didn't come to my wedding."

"I just got back from the war," I explained.

"Oh, okay," she said. "Well, I've had a really rough time, Nick, and now I don't trust much."

I waited for her to say more, but she stayed quiet. So, I changed the subject and asked about her daughter.

"I guess she talks and eats and everything…"

"Yes," she replied. Then she looked at me and said, "Listen, Nick, let me tell you what I said when my daughter was born. Do you want to hear it?"

"I would love to hear it," I replied.

"It'll show you how I feel about things now. She was less than an hour old when Tom wasn't even there. I woke up from the medicine feeling completely alone. I asked the nurse right away if it was a boy or a girl. She told me it was a girl, and I turned my head and cried. 'Okay,' I said, 'I'm glad it's a girl. I hope she'll be naive and innocent. That's the best thing a girl can be in this world, a beautiful little innocent.'"

"You see, I think everything is awful anyway," she continued, sounding very sure. "Everyone thinks so, even the smartest people. And I know. I've been everywhere, seen everything, and done every-thing." Her eyes darted around. "Experienced! Oh boy, I'm so expe-rienced!"

As soon as she stopped talking, I realized that what she had said wasn't sincere. However, she put on a smile. I could tell it wasn't a real smile though.

~

INSIDE, the red room was filled with light. Tom and Miss Baker sat on opposite ends of a long couch, and she read a magazine to him out loud. As she turned a page, her slender arm muscles fluttered.

When we entered, she motioned for us to be quiet with a raised hand.

"To be continued," she said, tossing the magazine on the table, "in the next issue."

She fidgeted, moving her knee restlessly, and then stood up.

"It's ten o'clock," she said, looking up at the ceiling as if checking the time. "Time for this good girl to go to bed."

"Jordan is playing in a tournament tomorrow," Daisy explained. "It's over in Westchester."

"Oh, so you're Jordan Baker."

I knew why her face looked familiar—I had seen it in sports pictures hanging in fancy clubs. I had heard a not-so-nice story about her too, but I didn't remember what it was.

"Good night," she said softly. "Wake me up at eight, please."

"If you get up."

"I will. Good night, Mr. Carraway. I'll see you soon."

"Of course you will," Daisy agreed. "Actually, I think I'll try to set up a marriage for you two. Come over often, Nick, and I'll try to bring you closer together by locking you in closets or sending you on boat trips, and stuff like that—"

"Good night," said Miss Baker from the stairs. "I didn't hear anything you just said."

"She's a nice girl," said Tom after a moment. "They shouldn't let her travel around the country like this."

"Who shouldn't?" asked Daisy coldly.

"Her family."

"Her family is just one really old aunt. Besides, Nick will take care of her, won't you, Nick? She's going to spend a lot of weekends here this summer. I think being at home will be good for her."

Daisy and Tom looked at each other silently for a moment.

"Is she from New York?" I asked quickly.

"No, she's from Louisville. We grew up together there. We have a special connection."

"Did you have a serious talk with Nick on the porch?" Tom suddenly asked.

"Did we?" Daisy looked at me. "I can't remember, but I think we talked about the Nordic race. Yes, I'm pretty sure we did. It kind of sneaked up on us and before we knew it—"

"Don't believe everything you hear, Nick," he warned.

I casually replied that I hadn't heard anything at all, and a few minutes later, I stood up to leave. They walked me to the door and stood together in a bright patch of light. Just as I was starting my car, Daisy called out, "Wait!"

"I forgot to ask you something, and it's important. We heard a rumor that you were engaged to a girl from the West."

"That's right," Tom kindly confirmed. "We heard that you were engaged."

"That's funny. I'm too poor to be engaged."

"But we heard it from three different people, so it must be true," said Daisy.

I knew exactly what they were referring to, but I wasn't even a little bit engaged. The fact that gossips had spread rumors was one of the reasons I had come East.

26   I drove away feeling confused and a little annoyed, but also somewhat touched by their interest. It made them seem less rich and distant. As I drove away, all I could think was how I wished Daisy had taken her daughter and left Tom. His behavior was unacceptable. It wasn't that surprising to hear that he had a woman in New York, but it was more unexpected that he was bothered by a book. It seemed like something was causing him to toy with old ideas, as if his confidence in his physical self was no longer enough for his strong-willed heart.

By the time I reached my property in West Egg, it was deep summer again. I parked my car. The wind had died down, leaving a clear and vibrant night. I could hear the insects buzzing in the trees. As I turned my head to watch a cat move across the moonlit landscape, I realized I wasn't alone. About fifty feet away, someone emerged from the shadow of my neighbor's big house. They stood with their hands in their pockets, gazing at the sparkling stars. The way they moved so casually and confidently on the lawn made me think it was Mr. Gatsby himself, coming out to claim his part of the night sky.

27   I wanted to talk to him, but he seemed like he wanted to be alone. He reached his arms out towards the water in a strange way. Even though I was far away, I thought I saw him shaking. I looked towards the sea and could only see a small green light in the distance, maybe from a dock. When I looked back, Gatsby was gone, and I was alone in the dark again.

CHAPTER

TWO

28 IN THE MIDDLE of a road that connects West Egg and New York, there is a part where the road quickly meets a train track. It's as if it wants to avoid a sad, lonely stretch of land. This area is called the "valley of ashes." It's a strange place where ashes blow all around and create little hills of ashes.

Above this gloomy land and the never-ending clouds of gray dust, you can see the eyes of Doctor T. J. Eckleburg. His eyes are blue and enormous, as big as a yardstick. They don't belong to a face, but are part of huge yellow glasses that have no nose behind them. A funny eye doctor painted them there as part of an advertisement to get more patients in Queens. However, he either went blind or forgot about them and left. Even though the add has been ruined by the weather over time, they keep watching over this sad dumping ground.

29 The valley of ashes has a dirty river on one side. Sometimes, a drawbridge goes up to let boats pass, and then people on the train have to stop and look at the gloomy view for a long time, maybe even half an hour. The wait is always at least one minute, and it was during one of these stops that I first saw Tom Buchanan's girlfriend.

Everyone made a big deal about him having a girlfriend. People didn't like that he would go to popular cafes with her, leave her at a table, and then go talk to other people. I was curious to see her, but I didn't really want to meet her. I ended up meeting her anyway. One afternoon, I went to New York with Tom on the train, and when we stopped by the ash heaps, he suddenly stood up, grabbed my arm, and literally made me get off the train.

"We're getting off," he insisted. "I want you to meet my girlfriend."

I think he'd had a lot to drink at lunch, and he was very determined to have me come with him. He didn't care if I had plans.

I walked behind him as we hopped over a short white fence by the train tracks. As we strolled, we felt the watchful eyes of Doctor Eckleburg looking down on us. Ahead, we saw a building that had a car repair garage. The sign said "Repairs. George B. Wilson. Cars bought and sold." Tom led me inside.

The inside was dull. The only car we could see was a dirty, unused Ford sitting in a dark corner. Suddenly, the owner of the garage appeared at the door of his office, wiping his hands with a rag. He was pale, weak, and slightly good-looking. When he saw us, a glimmer of hope shone in his light blue eyes.

"Hey, Wilson, my old buddy," said Tom, giving him a friendly pat on the shoulder. "How's business?"

"I can't complain," Wilson replied with a lack of confidence. "When are you going to sell me that car?"

"Next week. My man is working on it right now."

"He's pretty slow, isn't he?"

"No, he's not," Tom said coldly. "And if you feel that way, maybe I should sell it somewhere else after all."

"I didn't mean that," Wilson said quickly. "I just meant—"

His voice trailed off and Tom looked around the garage impatiently. Then I heard footsteps coming down the stairs, and soon a woman appeared in the doorway, blocking out the light. She was in her thirties and slightly plump, but she carried herself in a way that was pleasing. Her face, above a spotted dress, didn't have any special beauty, but she was lively. She smiled slowly and walked right through her husband, as if he wasn't even there, and shook hands with Tom, looking him straight in the eyes. Then she licked her lips and spoke to her husband in a soft, rough voice without turning around:

"Find some chairs, so people can sit down."

"Sure," Wilson agreed quickly and headed towards the small office. Meanwhile, his wife moved closer to Tom.

"I need to talk to you," Tom said seriously. "Get on the next train."

"Okay."

"I'll meet you by the newsstand downstairs."

She nodded and moved away from him, just as George Wilson appeared with two chairs from his office door.

We waited for her down the road, where we couldn't be seen.

"This place is awful," said Tom, making a disapproving face at the billboard with big eyes on it.

"Terrible," I agreed. "Does her husband know?" I asked.

"Wilson? He thinks she goes to visit her sister in New York. He's not very smart."

So Tom, his girlfriend, and I went to New York together, kind of. Mrs. Wilson sat in a different train car to keep up appearances with the fancy people from East Egg.

She changed into a brown dress when we arrived in New York. It was tight and showed off her wide hips. Tom helped her off the train. In the train station, she bought some magazines and beauty products. Then, we got in a fancy taxi and drove away from the crowded station into the sunny day. But right away, she leaned forward and tapped on the front window of the cab.

"I really want to get a dog," she said. "I want to have one in our apartment. Dogs are nice to have."

We backed up to an old man. He had a basket hanging from his neck that held a bunch of brand-new puppies.

"What kind of dogs are they?" Mrs. Wilson asked eagerly, leaning out the taxi window.

"They're all kinds. What kind are you looking for?"

"I want a police dog. Do you have any of those?" she asked. The man looked into the basket with uncertainty, reached in, and pulled out a squirming puppy by its neck.

"That's not a police dog," Tom remarked.

Mrs. Wilson said, full of enthusiasm. "How much does it cost?"

"That dog?" He looked at it admirably. "That dog will cost you ten dollars."

"Is it a boy or a girl?" she asked delicately.

"That dog? It's a boy."

"It's a girl," Tom stated firmly. "Here's your money."

34 We drove down Fifth Avenue, which was warm and calm on a sunny Sunday afternoon.

We drove through the city. Myrtle tugged at my sleeve.

"Come with us," she urged. "I'll call my sister Catherine. People say she's very pretty."

"Well, I want to, but..."

We continued driving, going back across the Park towards the west side of town. The taxi stopped at a tall building on 158th Street. Mrs. Wilson gathered her dog and the things she bought, and walked inside. She looked proud.

"I'm going to invite the McKees to come up," she said as we rode the elevator. "And, of course, I have to call my sister too."

35 The apartment was very small. It had a little living room, a little dining room, a little bedroom, and a bathroom. The living room was filled with big furniture that was too big for the room. It made it hard to walk around without tripping over it.

Mrs. Wilson was mostly concerned about her dog. She asked the elevator boy to get some straw and milk for the dog. The elevator boy also gave the dog some large, hard dog biscuits, which sat in the milk all afternoon and got all mushy. Meanwhile, Tom took out a bottle of whisky from a locked cabinet.

I don't drink often. The second time in my life I was drunk was that day.

More and more people started arriving at the apartment.

Tom's sister, Catherine, was a thin, fashionable woman around thirty years old. She had short, red hair and wore a lot of makeup. Her eyebrows were plucked and then drawn on again in a different way. She wore pottery bracelets on her arms that jingled when she moved. She acted as if she owned the place and looked at the furniture as if it belonged to her.

Mr. McKee was a thin, soft-spoken man who lived in the apartment below. He was a photographer. His wife was loud, tired-looking, attractive, and unpleasant. She proudly told me that her husband had taken photos of her 127 times since they got married.

Mrs. Wilson had changed her clothes earlier and was now wearing a fancy cream-colored dress. Along with her outfit, her personality had also changed. She acted like she was very important. Her laughter, movements, and statements became even more exaggerated as time went on. It felt like the room was getting smaller as she took up more space.

"Oh, my dear," she loudly told her sister, "most men will always try to cheat you. All they care about is money."

"Her name was Mrs. Eberhardt. She goes to people's houses to look at their feet."

Mrs. McKee complimented Mrs. Wilson by saying, "I really like your dress. It's adorable."

Mrs. Wilson responded by raising her eyebrow and saying, "It's just an old dress. I only wear it when I don't care how I look."

Suddenly, Tom Buchanan yawned loudly and stood up.

"You McKees should get some drinks," he said. "Myrtle, go get more ice and mineral water before everyone falls asleep."

"I already told that boy about the ice," Myrtle said with a frustrated look. "These people! You have to keep reminding them all the time."

She looked at me and laughed for no reason. Then she went into the kitchen to direct an imaginary team of chefs.

"I've done some nice things on Long Island," said Mr. McKee.

"We have two of them framed downstairs. One is called Montauk Point—The Gulls, and the other is called Montauk Point—The Sea," Tom replied.

Catherine, the sister, sat next to me on the couch.

"Do you live on Long Island too?" she asked.

"I live in West Egg."

"Really? I went to a party there about a month ago. It was at a man named Gatsby's. Do you know him?"

"I live next door to him."

"Well, they say he's related to Kaiser Wilhelm. That's where he gets all his money."

"Really?"

She nodded.

"I'm scared of him. I wouldn't want him to find out anything about me."

Just as I was absorbing this interesting information about my neighbor, Mrs. McKee suddenly pointed at Catherine:

"Chester, I think you could paint her," she blurted.

Mr. McKee said, "I would like to do more work on Long Island. I only need a chance to prove myself."

"Ask Myrtle," said Tom, laughing briefly. "She can introduce you around."

"Do what?" she asked, surprised.

Catherine whispered in my ear, leaning close to me:

"Neither of them can stand who they married. Why stay with someone you can't stand? They both need divorces."

I could tell Myrtle was listening.

"You see," Catherine said, "His wife is a Catholic and doesn't believe in divorce. She won't give Tom one."

That wasn't true.

"When they do get married," Catherine continued, "they plan to move out West for a while until things settle down."

"It would be best to go to Europe."

The sky outside the window was glowing. But then, Mrs. McKee's loud voice brought me back inside the room.

"I almost made a mistake too," she said with energy. "I ended up with, but a man who was beneath me had chased me for years."

"Yep, at least you didn't marry him," Myrtle Wilson agreed, nodding her head.

"I know I didn't," Mrs. McKee said proudly.

"Well, I did marry him," Myrtle said. "That's the difference between your situation and mine. I married George because I thought he was from a good family. He wasn't."

"You were really in love with him for a while," Catherine said.

"In love with him? No way!" Myrtle exclaimed, unable to believe it. "Who said I was in love with him?"

She pointed at me and everyone looked at me with narrow eyes.

"I was only crazy when I married him. I knew right away that I made a mistake. He borrowed someone's nicest suit to wear for the wedding, and he never even told me about it. When the man who he borrowed it from came to get it back, I cried."

"She should really leave him," Catherine told me. "They've been living above that garage for eleven years. And Tom is the first person she ever had a relationship with."

Everyone except Catherine kept asking for more whisky. Tom called downstairs for more sandwiches. I wanted to leave and walk towards the park in the soft evening light, but I always got pulled back into my seat. High above the city, our line of windows must have looked interesting. I saw someone looking up from the street. I felt connected and disconnected at the same time.

Myrtle sat next to me and started sharing the story of how she first met Tom.

"We met on the train. He was so well-dressed. I couldn't stop looking at him, but whenever he looked at me, I had to pretend I was interested in the advertisement above his head. When we arrived at the station, we hopped into a cab together. All I could think was 'You only live once! You only live once!'"

She turned to Mrs. McKee, and the room filled with her fake laughter.

"Oh, my dear," she exclaimed, "I'm going to give you this dress when I'm done with it. I have to get another one tomorrow. I need to make a list of all the things I have to get—an appointment for a massage and a hairstyling, a collar for the dog, a cute ashtray with a spring, and a black silk bow wreath for my mother's grave that will last all summer. I must write down the list so I won't forget all the things I need to do."

44 It was nine o'clock. Right after that, I checked my watch and saw that it was ten.

The small dog sat on the table. People appeared and disappeared, made plans to go somewhere, and then lost each other. They searched for each other and found each other just a few feet away. Close to midnight, Tom Buchanan and Mrs. Wilson stood face to face. They were loud. Then I heard:

"Daisy! Daisy! Daisy!" Mrs. Wilson shouted. "I'll say it whenever I want to! Daisy! Dai—"

With a quick and skillful move, Tom Buchanan hit her nose with his open hand.

45 It was morning when everything started to get chaotic. I heard loud voices. Among the confusion, I could hear someone crying out in pain. Mr. McKee woke up from his sleep and seemed confused. He tried to walk towards the door but stopped halfway and stared at the scene. His wife and Catherine were busy moving around the crowded room. There was someone on the couch, bleeding and trying to read a magazine about towns. It was a mess. Finally, Mr. McKee continued on his way out the door, and I followed him, grabbing my hat from the chandelier.

While we were in the elevator, Mr. McKee suggested that we

should have lunch together someday. I asked him where he wanted to go and he said anywhere.

Then, I found myself half asleep in the cold part of the train station. I was waiting for the four o'clock train, staring at the morning newspaper.

CHAPTER

THREE

46   Dᴜʀɪɴɢ ᴛʜᴇ sᴜᴍᴍᴇʀ ɴɪɢʜᴛs, I heard music coming from my neighbor's house. People were all over the house and in the gardens. In the afternoon, I saw his guests jumping into the water or tanning on his beach. His two motorboats were docked nearby. On weekends, his fancy Rolls-Royce became like a big bus, taking people to and from the city from morning until late at night. By Monday, eight workers and a gardener shaped up the mansion once more.

    By Friday, five crates of oranges and lemons would be delivered. A butler used a fancy juicer to prepare for the party.

47   Once in a while, a group of people who prepare food and drinks would come to Gatsby's big garden. Inside, there would be a buffet of food and a stocked bar.

    By seven o'clock, the band had arrived. It wasn't just a small group, but a big group with lots of different instruments like oboes, trombones, saxophones, and drums. Cars rolled in and everyone was dressed in fancy clothes. There was chatter and laughter among the guests.

48   As the sky gets darker, the lights get brighter. Music starts play-

ing. Everyone's voices become louder and more joyful. There is talking, laughter, and beautiful people.

Suddenly, a girl dressed in shiny clothes takes a drink and dances. Everyone watches silently for a moment. Then the music changes to match her dance. People start talking again, spreading the rumor that she is a famous dancer. The party has officially started.

The first time I went to Gatsby's house, I was one of the few guests who received an invitation. Most people just went there on their own. Many guests would come and go without even meeting Gatsby.

But I was actually invited. One Saturday morning, a driver dressed in light blue brought me a formal note from Gatsby himself. The note said that it would be Gatsby's honor if I attended his "little party" that night. Gatsby had seen me before and had wanted to visit me earlier, but things had gotten in the way. The note was signed by Jay Gatsby in a very grand handwriting.

I dressed in white pants and a white shirt, and went to Gatsby's lawn a little after seven. I didn't know a single person.

When I got there, I tried to find Gatsby, but the people I asked seemed surprised. No one knew where he was. Feeling awkward, I went to the cocktail table in the garden. It was the only place where I could be alone without looking out of place.

I was so embarrassed and then Jordan Baker, the woman at Daisy's house, came out of the mansion. She stood at the top of the steps and looked down at the garden. She looked at me with boredom and pity.

I was relieved. I knew I needed to attach myself to someone.

"Hello!" I shouted, walking towards her. I sounded loud.

"I knew I would find you here," she said when I approached. "I remembered you live next door."

She held my hand without much feeling, as if she promised to take care of me soon.

Two girls approached Jordan about her golf tournament. She had lost in the finals the week before.

"You don't remember who we are," said one of the girls, "but we met you here about a month ago."

They spoke for a few moments.

"I like going to these parties," one girl said. "I always have a good time and it doesn't matter what I do. Last time I was here, my dress got torn on a chair. A guy asked for my name and address, and within a week, I got a package with a new evening gown from Croirier's."

"Did you keep it?" Jordan asked.

"Of course I did. It's a little big, so I'm having it altered. It's a two hundred and sixty-five dollar dress."

"Seems like an odd thing to do though," said the other girl. "I guess he wants to avoid trouble."

"Who?" I asked.

"Gatsby."

We all felt a shiver.

The talked about the various rumors they'd heard about him. They heard he was a German spy and that he killed someone.

"Oh, no," one girl disagreed. "He was in the American army during the war." She then commented on how mysterious he was.

We all turned and looked around for Gatsby.

Jordan and I ate dinner with a few other couples. We then got up to search for Gatsby.

I had never met him before and was rather nervous.

We looked around for Gatsby, but he wasn't there. We checked the bar and the porch, but no luck. Then we found a fancy door and went inside, ending up in a library that looked like it came from an old building in another country.

A man with big glasses, who seemed a little drunk, was sitting by a big table, staring at the books. When he saw us, he got excited and looked Jordan up and down.

"What do you think?" he asked quickly.

"About what?"

He pointed at the bookshelves.

"That. Actually, you don't need to check. I already did. They're real."

"The books?"

He nodded.

"They're really real. They even have pages. I thought they were just made of cardboard, but no, they're real. They have pages." He grabbed a book and showed it to us. "Look! It's a real book. I was fooled at first. This guy is amazing. It's a success. So detailed! So real! And he even knew not to cut the pages. But what did you expect?"

Thinking we wouldn't believe him, he hurried to the bookcases and came back with a book called Volume One of the Stoddard Lectures.

"Look!" he exclaimed triumphantly. "It's a real printed book. It fooled me. This guy is like a famous theater director, Belasco. It's amazing. So detailed! So lifelike! They even left the pages uncut. But what more do you want? What do you expect?"

He took the book back from me and placed it quickly back on the shelf. He muttered that if even one book was moved, the whole library might collapse.

"Who brought you here?" he asked. "Or did you just come on your own? I was brought here. Most people were brought."

Jordan looked at him with interest and a smile but didn't answer.

"I was brought here by a lady named Mrs. Claud Roosevelt," he continued. "Do you know her? I met her somewhere last night. I've been drunk for about a week now, and I thought being in a library might help me sober up."

"Has it?" I asked.

"I think a little bit. It's hard to tell. I've only been here for an hour. Did I tell you about the books? They're real. They're—"

"Yes, you already told us," I interrupted.

We shook hands with him seriously, and then we went back outside.

Now there was dancing, singing, and performing.

Large glasses of champagne were served. The moon was high in the sky, and the Sound shimmered with silver reflections. The sound of the banjos played on the lawn.

I was sitting with Jordan Baker at a table. There was a man around my age and a playful girl with us. She giggled uncontrollably at the slightest thing. I had two glasses of champagne at that point. The man looked at me with a grin.

"I feel like I've seen you before," he said politely. "Were you in the First Division during the war?"

"Yes," I replied excitedly. "I was in the Twenty-eighth Infantry."

"I was in a military unit called the Sixteenth until June 1918. I knew I had seen you somewhere before."

We talked briefly. He mentioned that he lived nearby and had just bought a hydroplane he planned to test in the morning.

"Do you want to come with me, old sport? We can stay close to the shore by the Sound."

"What time?" I asked.

"Any time that works best for you."

I almost asked for his name, but then Jordan looked over and smiled.

Then, I turned back to my new friend. "This is a great party. I'm waiting to meet a man named Gatsby. He sent his driver with an invitation to me." For a moment, he looked at me as if he didn't understand.

"I'm Gatsby," he said suddenly.

"What!" I exclaimed. "Oh, I'm sorry."

"I thought you knew, old sport. I'm afraid I haven't been a very good host."

He smiled kindly, more than kindly. It was a rare smile that made me feel safe and welcome. It felt as if he was looking at the whole world for a moment, and then focused on me with a strong glance. He understood me the way I wanted to be understood, believed in me as I wish others would, and made me feel like he saw the best version of myself. But then the smile disappeared, and I saw a young man in his thirties who spoke in a fancy way that almost seemed silly. Even before he introduced himself, I could tell that he was choosing his words carefully.

Just as Mr. Gatsby told us who he was, a butler rushed over to tell him that he had a call from Chicago. He excused himself with a small bow and said we could ask for anything we needed. Then he left, promising to join us again later.

As soon as he was gone, I turned to Jordan and expressed my surprise. I had expected Mr. Gatsby to be an older, plump man.

"Who is he?" I asked. "Do you know?"

"He's simply a man named Gatsby."

"Where is he from? And what does he do?"

"Now that we're talking about it," she replied with a tired smile. "He once said he went to Oxford. But I don't believe him."

"Why not?"

"I don't know," she insisted, "I just don't think he really went there."

Her tone reminded me of the other girl's claim that he had killed someone. It made me even more curious. I wondered where he came from. I was also from a small town, so I didn't think that young men could just appear out of nowhere and buy a grand house on Long Island Sound.

"Anyway, he throws big parties. I prefer them to small parties. Small parties don't have any privacy."

Suddenly, the band leader spoke on the microphone.

"Ladies and gentlemen," he announced. "By Mr. Gatsby's request, we will now perform Mr. Vladmir Tostoff's newest composition, which made a big splash at Carnegie Hall in May. If you read the news, you know it caused quite a sensation." He smiled with a friendly arrogance and added, "What a sensation!" Everyone burst into laughter.

"The piece is called 'Vladmir Tostoff's Jazz History of the World!'" he said happily.

I saw Gatsby standing alone on the steps. He was looking around at the different groups of people with a smile on his face. His skin was tan and his hair looked neatly trimmed. There was nothing scary or strange about him. I wondered if the fact that he wasn't drinking made him stand out from his guests. As everyone got sillier and louder, Gatsby seemed to become more formal. After the "Jazz History of the World" ended, couples were being playful and leaning on each other. They were even falling into people, knowing that someone would catch them. But no one leaned on Gatsby, and no girl's bobbed haircut touched his shoulder. He wasn't part of the singing groups that formed either.

"I'm sorry."

Gatsby's butler appeared suddenly next to us.

"Miss Baker?" he asked. "I'm sorry, but Mr. Gatsby would like to talk to you alone."

"With me?" she said, surprised.

"Yes, ma'am."

She stood up slowly. She followed the butler to the house. I noticed she was wearing her fancy dress. She always wore sporty clothes. She moved with a lightness, as if she had first learned how to walk on golf courses on cool mornings.

I was all by myself and I decided to go inside.

The room was filled with people. A young woman played the piano, crying for some reason, and then singing.

"She had an argument with a man who claims to be her husband," a girl next to me explained.

I looked around and saw a lot of arguing. There were little fights here and there. Everyone tried to figure out when and how to get home.

Many wives were carried away, kicking and screaming.

I stood in the hallway waiting for my hat. I saw Jordan Baker and Gatsby walking out of the library. Gatsby seemed excited as he talked to Jordan, but his mood quickly changed. He noticed people coming toward him.

Jordan's friends on the porch were calling for her to hurry up. However, she stayed for a moment to shake hands with Gatsby.

I joined the remaining guests who were gathered around Gatsby. I wanted to explain that I had been looking for him earlier in the evening. I wanted to apologize for not recognizing him in the garden.

"Don't worry about it," he said eagerly. "Don't give it another thought, my friend." He was very kind and reminded him to meet him for the hydroplane ride at 9:00AM.

Just then, the butler appeared behind him and said, "Philadelphia is calling for you, sir."

"Alright, in a little bit. Tell them I'll come right away... Good night."

"Good night."

Then, I saw not far from the driveway there was quite a bit of craziness. In the ditch beside the road, a brand-new car was resting on its side. It had lost a wheel in a violent accident and was now getting a lot of attention from a few curious drivers. But because they had left their cars blocking the road, the noise of angry drivers in the back had been filling the air for a while, making the scene even more chaotic.

"I'm not sure how all that happened," said Owl Eyes, the man from the library, giving up on the whole thing. "I don't know much about driving—almost nothing. It happened, and that's all I know."

"Well, if you're not a good driver, you shouldn't try driving at night."

The bystanders were in awe.

"You don't get it," said the person responsible. "I wasn't driving. There's another man in the car."

The shock that followed this statement was expressed with a long "Ah-h-h!" as the door of the car slowly swung open. A very messy figure got out of the car. The person stood swaying a bit.

He took a deep breath and stood up tall, determined to ask a question.

"Can you tell me where to find a gas station?"

A bunch of men, some of them in a better situation than him, explained that the wheel was no longer connected to the car.

"Maybe try backing up," he suggested. "Put it in reverse."

"But the wheel is off!"

He paused for a moment.

"It can't hurt to try," he said.

The loud horns were making a lot of noise, so I turned and headed home. I looked back once. There was a small moon shining over Gatsby's house, making the night beautiful as always, despite the laughter and noise coming from his lively garden. Suddenly, I felt a sense of emptiness coming from the windows and the big doors, as if the host standing on the porch was completely alone, saying goodbye.

~

As I READ through what I have written so far, I realize that I made it seem like the events on those three nights, which were several weeks apart, were all that mattered to me. But in reality, those events were just minor moments in a busy summer.

Most of the time, I worked. In the early morning, the sun made my shadow stretch to the west as I hurried down the big streets of lower New York to the Probity Trust. I knew the other people who worked there by their first names, and ate lunch with them in small, crowded restaurants. We ate well. I had a brief romance, but her brother gave me dirty look. When she went on vacation, we stopped talking.

After work, I'd go to the Yale Club or the library. I could focus on my work there. If the evening was nice, I walked back to the train station to return home.

I started to like New York City, especially when it was nighttime. It felt exciting and full of adventure. There was a lot of mystery and fun. But I would also feel a sense of loneliness. I would see other young people like me walking around. Sometimes I'd have dinner alone. It felt like many of us were wasting the most special moments of the night and our lives.

At eight o'clock, when the city was busy, I would feel a heaviness in my heart. The taxis would be filled with people talking and laughing, and I wished I could join in on their excitement.

In the summer, I saw Jordan Baker again after losing sight of her for a while. I was happy to hang out with her because she was famous for playing golf. But then, I started to feel something more. It wasn't love, but I was curious about her.

She always seemed bored, but I was interested in her.

One day, while we were at a party in Warwick, she left a car that wasn't hers outside in the rain with the top down. Later, she lied about it. That reminded me of a story about her that I couldn't remember before. During her first important golf competition, there was a big disagreement. People said she cheated by moving her ball to a better position. It was almost a scandal, but then it went away. One of the people who saw it happen took back what they said, and the other witness admitted they might have been wrong. I couldn't forget about that incident and her name together.

Jordan Baker didn't like clever men. She was always being dishonest. She didn't like being at a disadvantage, so she started lying when she was young to keep up appearances.

But it didn't bother me. I didn't blame her for being dishonest—I was just a little sorry, and then I forgot about it. We had an interesting conversation about driving during the house party. It all started because Jordan passed some workmen very closely and our car bumped into one of them.

"You're a really bad driver," I said. "Either you need to be more careful, or you shouldn't drive at all."

"I am careful," she replied.

"No, you're not."

"Well, other people are," she said with a light tone.

"What does that have to do with anything?"

"They'll stay out of my way," she insisted. "It takes two people to have an accident."

"But what if you meet someone who is just as careless as you?"

"I hope that never happens," she said. "I hate careless people. That's why I like you."

Her eyes, tired from the sun, looked straight ahead, but she had changed our relationship. For a moment, I thought I was in love with her. But I am a slow thinker and have many rules that stop me from doing what I want. I knew that I needed to figure things out at home before anything else. I used to send letters once a week signed with "Love, Nick," and all I could think about was how the girl who played tennis had a little bit of sweat above her lip. There was an unspoken agreement that needed to be gently ended before I could be free.

Everyone thinks they have at least one good quality, and mine is honesty. I'm one of the few people I know who can say that.

CHAPTER

FOUR

 ON SUNDAY MORNING, when bells rang in the nearby villages, people went to Gatsby's house and had a great time on his lawn.

The young ladies whispered, "He's a bootlegger," as they moved between his cocktails and flowers. "Once, he even killed a man who knew he was related to important people. Pass me a rose, dear, and pour some last drops into my fancy glass."

During that summer, I made a timetable and wrote down the names of the people who visited Gatsby's house. The timetable is old and falling apart now, but it says "This schedule in effect July 5th, 1922." I can still read the names, and they will tell you more about the people who enjoyed Gatsby's hospitality without knowing much about him. All of them were very rich.

 For example, Clarence Endive was from the nearby area of East Egg. I remember he visited once, wearing white knee-length pants. He got into a fight with a man named Etty in the garden. Some people came from further out on the island, like the Cheadles, the O.R.P. Schraeders, the Stonewall Jackson Abrams from Georgia, and the Fishguards and the Ripley Snells. Mr. Snell ended up going to jail three days after being at the party. He was so drunk on the driveway that Mrs. Ulysses Swett's car ran over his right hand. The Dancies were also there, along with S.B. Whitebait, who was over sixty years old, Maurice A. Flink, the Hammerheads, Beluga the tobacco importer, and Beluga's girls.

People from West Egg attended as well. There were the Poles, the Mulreadys, Cecil Roebuck, Cecil Schoen, Gulick the State Senator, Newton Orchid who controlled Films Par Excellence, Eckhaust, Clyde Cohen, Don S. Schwartz (the son), and Arthur McCarty. They were all involved in the movie industry in some way. The Catlips, the Bembergs, and G. Earl Muldoon, the brother of a man who later killed his wife, were there too. Da Fontano the promoter also came, along with Ed Legros, James B. (known as "Rot-Gut") Ferret, the De Jongs, and Ernest Lilly. They came to gamble, and when Ferret went into the garden, it meant he had lost all his money, and the Associated Traction company would have to make a profitable recovery the next day.

There was a man who came to visit often at the house. Peopl started to call him "the boarder." It seemed like he didn't have any other place to live.

That summer, many people came to Gatsby's house.

One morning in July, Gatsby's beautiful car drove up to my house and honked its horn, playing a nice song. It was the first time he'd visited me. I had gone to two of his parties and used his beach as he invited me.

"Good morning, old sport. Let's have lunch together today, and I thought we could ride up together," he said.

He noticed me admiring his car.

"Isn't it beautiful, old friend?" He hopped off the car to give me a better view. "Have you seen it before?"

I had seen it. Everyone had seen it. It was a pretty cream color, shiny with metal, and filled with big boxes and windshields that reflected the sunlight. Sitting inside, surrounded by layers of glass, it felt like being in a green leather greenhouse. We started driving towards town.

"Listen, my friend," he suddenly burst out, "what do you really think of me?"

Feeling a bit surprised, I began to give simple answers.

"Well, let me tell you something about my life," he interrupted. "I don't want you to have the wrong idea about me from all the gossip you hear."

So he was aware of the strange rumors that spread in his house.

"I'll tell you the truth," he said with confidence. "I come from a rich family in the Midwest. I grew up in America but went to school in Oxford, which is a family tradition."

He glanced at me and I understood why Jordan Baker thought he was lying. He spoke quickly. "My whole family died and I received a lot of money."

His voice was serious.

"After that, I lived like a wealthy person in all the big cities of Europe, like Paris, Venice, and Rome. I collected jewels, hunted wild animals, did some painting. I was trying to forget my sad past."

I tried hard not to burst out laughing. It all seemed wild and strange.

"Then came the war, my friend. It was a big relief, and I tried really hard to die, but it seemed like I had a special kind of luck. When the war started, I became a first lieutenant. I led my machine-gun group into the Argonne Forest, and we went so far ahead that the infantry couldn't get through on either side of us. We stayed there for two days and two nights with 130 men and 16 guns. Because of my bravery, I got promoted to major, and all the countries in the Allies gave me gifts. Even Montenegro, a tiny country by the Adriatic Sea!"

He smiled and nodded as if remembering the history and struggles of little Montenegro. It was amazing to me. He showed me a medal with a ribbon attached to it. I was shocked. I read, "Major Jay Gatsby, For Being Extremely Brave."

"Here's something I always have with me. A memento from my time at Oxford. This picture was taken in Trinity Quad—a place with many tall towers. In the photo, there are a few young men wearing blazers, just hanging out in an archway. The guy on my left is now the Earl of Doncaster."

The picture showed Gatsby, looking a bit younger, holding a cricket bat.

And it was all true. I imagined the tiger skins blazing in his palace by the Grand Canal. I pictured him opening a chest full of rubies, their red glow soothing his broken heart.

"Today, I'm going to ask you to do something important," he said, putting away his souvenirs. "He paused. "You'll hear about it this afternoon."

"During lunch?"

"No, this afternoon. I found out that you're going to have tea with Miss Baker."

"Do you mean you're in love with Miss Baker?"

"No, old sport, I'm not. But Miss Baker kindly agreed to talk to you about this matter."

I had no clue what "this matter" was, but I was more annoyed than interested. I didn't invite Jordan for tea to discuss Mr. Jay Gatsby. I was wondering what she was going to ask me.

He didn't say anything else. He became more proper as we got closer to the city. After that, we entered the valley of ashes. I saw Mrs. Wilson pumping gas with lots of energy as we passed by the garage.

The car was easy to spot. A police officer on a motorcycle pulled up next to us.

"It's okay, old sport," Gatsby called out. We slowed down, and he showed the policeman a white card from his wallet.

"You're good," the policeman agreed, tipping his hat. "I'll remember you next time, Mr. Gatsby. Excuse me!"

"What was that about?" I asked.

"I did a favor for the police commissioner once, so he sends me a Christmas card every year."

We crossed the big bridge into the city.

A sad procession passed by us, filled with flowers. There were carriages with closed blinds and some happier carriages for friends. The friends looked at us sadly, with eyes that showed they were from a faraway place. I was glad to see that Gatsby's fancy car was part of their serious day. While we were crossing the island, a fancy car passed us. It was driven by a white chauffeur and had three stylish African American people inside.

The city always made me feel as though anything could happen.

LATER ON, I met up with Gatsby again for lunch in a cool underground room on 42nd Street. I saw Gatsby talking to another man in the waiting area.

"Mr. Carraway, this is my friend Mr. Wolfshiem," Gatsby said.

A small Jewish man, with a flat nose and hair sticking out of his nostrils, looked up and stared at me. In the dim light, I finally saw his small eyes.

"--So I looked at him," Mr. Wolfshiem said, shaking my hand firmly, "and guess what I did?"

"What?" I asked politely.

But it seemed he wasn't talking to me. He let go of my hand and focused his attention on Gatsby.

"I gave the money to Katspaugh and told him, 'Don't pay him anything until he stops talking.' And he stopped right then and there."

Gatsby put his arm around each of us and led us into the restaurant. Mr. Wolfshiem stopped his story.

"Would you care for highballs?" the head waiter asked.

"This is a nice restaurant," Mr. Wolfshiem commented. "But I prefer the one across the street!"

"Yes, highballs," agreed Gatsby, and then he said to Mr. Wolfshiem, "It's too hot there."

"Hot and small, indeed," added Mr. Wolfshiem, "but it's full of memories."

"What place is that?" I asked.

"The old Metropole."

"The old Metropole," Mr. Wolfshiem muttered sadly. "Filled with people who are no longer here. Filled with friends who are gone forever."

Mr. Wolfshiem turned to me, showing some interest. He said, "I heard you were looking for a business connection."

I was surprised. Gatsby spoke up for me:

"Oh no," he exclaimed, "this is just a friend. We'll talk about that some other time, as I mentioned."

"I apologize," said Mr. Wolfshiem, "I mistook you for someone else."

A delicious meal was served, and Mr. Wolfshiem, forgetting the old Metropole, began to eat with gusto. His eyes, however, scanned the room slowly. I think if I hadn't been there, he would have taken a quick look under our table.

"Listen, old sport," Gatsby leaned in closer to me, "I'm sorry if I upset you this morning in the car."

That smile appeared again, but this time I resisted it.

"I don't like secrets," I replied, "and I don't understand why you can't be straightforward and tell me what you want. Why does it all have to go through Miss Baker?"

"Oh, it's nothing sneaky," he said. "Miss Baker is a great athlete, you know, and she wouldn't do anything wrong."

Suddenly, he checked the time, stood up quickly, and left the room in a hurry, leaving me with Mr. Wolfshiem at the table.

"He has to make a phone call," Mr. Wolfshiem said, watching him go. "Great guy, isn't he? Handsome and a true gentleman."

"Yes."

"He went to a fancy college called Oxford."

"Oh!"

"He attended Oxford College in England. Have you heard of it?"

"I have."

"It's one of the most famous colleges in the world."

"How long have you known Gatsby?" I asked.

"For a few years," he answered happily. "I met him shortly after the war. But after talking with him for an hour, I knew he was a well-mannered man. I thought to myself, 'He's the kind of man you'd like to introduce to your family.' " He paused. "I see you're looking at my cuff buttons."

I hadn't been, but now I was. They were made of ivory that seemed oddly familiar.

"They're the finest human molars," he told me.

"Well!" I examined them. "That's a very interesting idea."

"Yeah." He rolled up his sleeves under his coat. "Yeah, Gatsby is very respectful of women. He would never even look at a friend's wife."

When Gatsby returned to the table, Mr. Wolfshiem quickly finished his coffee and stood up.

"I had a nice lunch," he said, "and I'm going to leave now before I stay too long."

He shook our hands and walked away.

"Sometimes he gets emotional," Gatsby explained. "Today is one of those days. He's quite a character in New York—always on Broadway."

"Who is he, though? Is he an actor?"

"No. He's a gambler." Gatsby paused, then said calmly, "He's the man who cheated in the World Series in 1919."

"He rigged the World Series?" I repeated.

I couldn't believe it. I knew that the World Series in 1919 was rigged. I never thought that one man could play with the trust of fifty million people, like a burglar trying to open a safe.

"Why did he do that?" I asked after a moment.

"He saw an opportunity," Gatsby replied.

"Why isn't he in trouble?"

"They can't catch him, old sport. He's clever."

I insisted on paying the bill. Then, I noticed Tom Buchanan in the crowded room.

"Come with me for a moment," I said. "I need to greet someone."

When Tom saw us, he hurried over to us.

"Where have you been?" he asked eagerly. "Daisy is angry because you haven't called."

"This is Mr. Gatsby, Mr. Buchanan."

They quickly shook hands, and Gatsby's face showed a tense, unfamiliar look of discomfort.

"How have you been?" Tom asked me. "Why did you come all the way here to have lunch?"

"I had lunch with Mr. Gatsby."

I turned to face Mr. Gatsby, but he was no longer there.

ONE OCTOBER DAY IN 1917—

(said Jordan Baker that afternoon, sitting up straight in a chair at the Plaza Hotel)

—I was walking from one place to another, partly on the sidewalks and partly on the lawns. I liked walking on the lawns because I had shoes from England with rubber knobs on the soles that gripped the soft ground. I also wore a new plaid skirt that fluttered a little in the wind. Whenever this happened, the red, white, and blue flags in front of the houses stood tall and seemed to scold, saying tut-tut-tut-tut, in a disapproving manner.

Daisy Fay's house had the biggest lawn. She was only eighteen, which was two years older than me. Daisy was the most popular girl in Louisville. She always wore white and drove a little white car. Her phone rang all day with excited young officers from a nearby army camp. They all wanted to get to know Daisy.

That morning, as I passed by her house, her white car was parked on the curb. She was sitting in it with a lieutenant who I had never seen before. They were so engaged in each other that she didn't notice me until I was right next to them.

"Hey, Jordan," she called out. "Come over here."

I felt honored that she wanted to talk to me because I admired her more than any of the older girls. As I approached, I noticed the young officer seated by her. The officer looked at Daisy in a way that every girl dreams of being looked at. It was romantic and I've always remembered that moment. The officer's name was Jay Gatsby, and it was over four years before I saw him again. Even when I met him on Long Island, I didn't realize it was the same man.

That happened in 1917. The next year, I had a few boys who liked me, and I started playing in tournaments, so I didn't see Daisy very often. She hung out with older people. There were rumors going around about her. Someone said she tried to run away, but was stopped by her mother. Afterward, she stopped hanging around with soldiers and started spending time with a few young men in town who couldn't join the army.

By the following fall, she was happy again, just as happy as before. She married Tom Buchanan from Chicago. The wedding was grand. He rented out the entire hotel and gave her a necklace with pearls worth three hundred and fifty thousand dollars.

I was one of the bridesmaids. I went into her room half an hour before the dinner, and I found her lying on her bed, looking beautiful in her dress with flowers, but she was also very drunk. She had a bottle of wine in one hand and a letter in the other.

"What's wrong, Daisy?"

I was really scared, I have to admit.

She took the pearls out of a trash can. She asked me to tell everyone that Daisy has changed her mind. She begged me to say: 'Daisy has changed her mind!'"

She started crying—crying and crying. I hurried out and found her mother's maid, and we locked the door and put her in a cold bath. She wouldn't let go of this letter she had. She brought it into the tub with her and crumpled it into a wet ball.

But she didn't say anything else. Half an hour later, when we left the room, she had the pearls around her neck and the incident was over. The next day at five o'clock, she married Tom Buchanan.

She was crazy about Tom. After their honeymoon, I saw her. She'd have a dreamy look on her face. It was sweet to see them together, and it made you laugh in a quiet way. That was in August. A week after, Tom had a car accident on the Ventura road. He hit a wagon and the car's front wheel came off. The girl who was with him also made it into the news because she broke her arm. She worked as a maid in the hotel they had stayed in for their honeymoon.

The following April, Daisy had her daughter, and they went to France for a year. Then they returned to Chicago to settle down. Daisy was well-liked in Chicago, as you know. They hung out with a fast crowd, all young, rich, and wild, but Daisy maintained a flawless reputation. Maybe because she never drank.

Well, a few weeks ago, she heard the name Gatsby again after a long time. It was when I asked you if you knew Gatsby in West Egg. After you left, she came into my room and woke me up. She asked, "Who is Gatsby?" When I described him, she said with a strange voice that it must be the man she used to know. It wasn't until then that I realized this Gatsby was the officer in her white car.

After Jordan Baker finished telling me all of this, we left the Plaza and were driving through Central Park.

"I thought it was a strange coincidence," I said.

"But it wasn't a coincidence at all. Gatsby bought that house so that Daisy would live across the bay."

Then I realized that on that June night, it wasn't just the stars he was reaching for. It was her.

"He wants to know," Jordan continued, "if you can invite Daisy to your house one afternoon and then let him come over."

He waited for a long time before asking such a small favor. He bought a big house where he shined bright lights for anyone passing by--all so he could come over to someone else's garden one afternoon.

"He's scared. He's waited so long, and he thought you might get mad. You know, he's tough on the surface," she explained.

Something was bothering me. I asked, "Why didn't he ask you to help set up a meeting?"

"He wants her to see his house," she said. "And your house is right next door. I think he hoped she would show up at one of his parties one night," Jordan continued, "but she never did. When I mentioned that you were a close friend of Tom's, he almost gave up on the idea. He doesn't know much about Tom, although he claims he's read a newspaper from Chicago for years just to catch a glimpse of Daisy's name."

It was nighttime. I put my arm around Jordan's shoulder and pulled her closer to me. I asked her if she wanted to have dinner. I liked her.

"Daisy should have something in her life," Jordan whispered to me.

"Does she want to see Gatsby?"

"Don't tell her right away. Gatsby doesn't want her to know. You're supposed to invite her for tea."

Unlike Gatsby and Tom Buchanan, I didn't have a special girl in my life. She smiled with her tired mouth. I pulled her closer to my face.

CHAPTER

FIVE

94 WHEN I GOT BACK HOME to West Egg that night, Gatsby's house was so bright, with every floor and room lit up.

At first, I thought there was another party happening, but as my taxi drove away, I saw Gatsby walking towards me on his lawn.

"Your place looks amazing, like the World's Fair," I said.

"Does it?" He looked at it without much passion. "I've been looking into some of the rooms from the outside. Enough of that though. Let's go to Coney Island, old sport. I have a car."

"It's too late."

"Well, maybe we can swim in the pool? I haven't used it all summer."

"I need to go to bed."

"Okay."

He waited, looking at me with excitement he was trying to hide.

"I talked to Miss Baker," I said after a moment. "I'm going to call Daisy tomorrow and invite her here for tea."

"Oh, that's not necessary," he said casually. "I don't want to trouble you."

"What day works for you?"

"What day would work for you?" he quickly corrected me. "I don't want to bother you."

"How about the day after tomorrow?" I suggested.

He thought about it. Then he said, "I need to cut the grass."

We both looked at the grass. It was messy.

"Also," He struggled to find the right words. "I have a small business on the side, a sort of extra job, you know. And I thought that if you don't make much money, this might interest you."

Looking back, I realize that under different circumstances, that conversation could have been a turning point in my life. I thanked him, but had to get to bed.

"I have a lot to do," I said. "Thank you, but I can't take on more work."

"You wouldn't have to do any business with Wolfshiem." He seemed to think that I was avoiding the "connection" mentioned at lunch. He waited for a moment and then went home.

The evening left me feeling light and happy. The next morning, I called Daisy and invited her to come for tea and I told her not to bring Tom.

The day we agreed upon was filled with pouring rain. At eleven o'clock, a man in a raincoat, dragging a lawn mower, knocked on my front door. He said Mr. Gatsby had sent him to cut my grass.

In addition to this, Gatsby all but had an entire florist's shop delivered to my house.

An hour later, Gatsby rushed in wearing a white suit, shiny shirt, and gold tie. He looked tired and had dark circles under his eyes. "Do you have everything you need, like tea?"

I took him to the pantry, where he seemed a bit disappointed by the twelve lemon cakes brought from the bakery.

"Will these work?" I asked.

"Of course, of course! They're great!" he said, but his voice sounded empty. He quietly added, "...old sport."

Gatsby waited and waited, but then suddenly said he was going to go home.

"Why?" I asked.

"No one is coming for tea. It's too late!" He checked his watch as if he had something very important to do. "I can't wait any longer."

"Don't be silly. It's about to be 4:00pm."

Feeling miserable, he sat down again, as if I had pushed him. Finally, a car pulled into the driveway with Daisy. She was wearing a lavender hat with three corners. She came to my door with a bright, happy smile.

"Is this really where you live, my dear one?"

She looked so nice.

99 She whispered in my ear. "Why did I have to come alone?"

"Tell your driver to go far away and come back in an hour."

"Come back in an hour, Ferdie." Then she said quietly, "His name is Ferdie."

We walked inside. The living room where Gatsby had been was empty. We heard a gentle knock at the door. Gatsby stood in a puddle of water, staring.

With his hands still in his pockets, he walked by me. He disappeared into the living room. For about half a minute, there was silence. Then I heard:

"I'm really happy to see you again."

There was a pause.

100 Gatsby was standing by the fireplace. He leaned against the fireplace mantel and nearly knocked a small clock over.

"I'm sorry about the clock," Gatsby apologized.

I could feel my face turning red. I couldn't think of anything to say.

"It's an old clock," I said, sounding foolish.

"We haven't seen each other in a long time," Daisy said, matter-of-factly.

"It's been five years since November," Gatsby replied.

101 In the midst of the happy chaos of tea and treats, things started to feel more comfortable. I stood up to give them time together. Gatsby stopped me.

"This is a big mistake," he said sadly.

"You're just embarrassed, that's all," I told him. "Daisy is embarrassed too. You're acting childish," I snapped. "You're being rude. Don't leave her in there all alone."

He raised his hand to silence me, gave me an annoyed look I won't forget. He went back inside.

I walked out of the house through the back way, just like Gatsby had done earlier. I hurried towards a big, dark tree with lots of leaves that protected me from the rain. It was pouring again, and my nicely trimmed lawn, taken care of by Gatsby's gardener, had tiny muddy spots and old marshes. There wasn't much to see from under the tree, except for Gatsby's huge house. I stared at it, like Kant staring at his church tower, for a long time, maybe around thirty minutes. A long time ago, a rich person built that house when everyone was crazy about that kind of style. There's a story that says this rich person promised to pay taxes for five years for all the small houses around if their owners agreed to put straw on their roofs. But when they said no, it broke his heart, and he got sick. His kids sold the house, and there was still a black wreath on the door. Even though Americans are willing to work hard for others, they have always been stubborn about being treated like peasants.

After thirty minutes, the sun came out again, and the grocer's car drove up to Gatsby's house with food for his servants' dinner. I was certain he wouldn't eat a bite. A maid started opening the windows on the upper floor of his house. She showed up in each window for a moment and spat into the garden while leaning out from the big central bay. It was time for me to go back. When it was raining, I heard their voices murmuring, getting louder at times with bursts of emotion. But now, in the quiet, I felt silence settle inside the house as well.

I went inside, making as much noise as possible in the kitchen without knocking over the stove. But I don't think they heard a thing. They were sitting at opposite ends of the couch, looking at each other as if a question had been asked or was hanging in the air.

All traces of embarrassment were gone. Daisy had tears all over her face, and when I entered, she got up and started wiping at it with her handkerchief in front of a mirror. But Gatsby had changed completely. He seemed to be glowing. There was a new sense of well-being radiating from him and filling the small room without him saying a word or making any triumphant gestures.

"Oh, hello, my old friend," he said, as if he hadn't seen me in years. For a moment, I thought he was going to shake my hand.

"The rain has stopped."

"Did it?" When he understood what I meant, that there were rays of sunshine in the room, he smiled and shared the news with Daisy. "Can you believe it? The rain has stopped."

"I'm happy, Jay." Her voice, filled with both sadness and unexpected joy, revealed her emotions.

"I want you and Daisy to come to my house," he said. "I'd like to show her around."

"Are you sure you want me to come?"

"Absolutely, old sport."

Daisy went upstairs to wash her face—I though about my shabby towels with embarrassment—while Gatsby and I waited on the lawn.

"Doesn't my house look impressive?" he asked. "Notice how the front catches the light."

I agreed that it looked amazing. I asked him what line of work he was in, he replied, "That's my business," before realizing it wasn't a suitable response.

"Oh, I've tried my hand at a few things," he corrected himself. "I worked in the pharmacy business and then the oil business. But I'm not in either one anymore." He looked at me more closely. "Does this mean you've been considering what I proposed the other night?"

Before I could reply, Daisy came out of the house and the shiny buttons on her dress caught the sunlight.

"That big house over there?" she exclaimed, pointing.

"Do you like it?"

"I love it, but I don't understand how you live there all by yourself."

"I always have interesting people filling it, day and night. People who do interesting things. Famous people."

Instead of taking the shortcut by the water, we went down the road and entered through the big entrance. Daisy admired different parts of the castle-like home.

We explored the rooms.

106 We went upstairs, through rooms filled with pretty pinks and purples and fresh flowers everywhere. We saw bedrooms, dressing rooms, and bathrooms with deep baths. In one room, there was a man in pajamas doing exercises. His name was Mr. Klipspringer, and we had seen him earlier on the beach.

Finally, we reached Gatsby's own rooms. There was a bedroom, a bathroom, and a study with fancy furniture. We sat down and drank a special drink called Chartreuse that Gatsby got from a cupboard.

Gatsby couldn't stop looking at Daisy. It seemed like everything in his house was more important to him because of her. Sometimes, he looked around in a confused way, as if nothing was real anymore because Daisy was there.

His bedroom was simple, except for a fancy gold set on the dresser. Daisy took a brush and brushed her hair, making Gatsby laugh.

"It's so funny," he said, laughing. "I can't... When I try to..."

107 He had gone through two different feelings and was now experiencing a third. First, he felt embarrassed, then extremely happy. He loved having her around.

After a short moment, he showed us his fancy collection of shirts and threw them in front of us, one by one. They were made of light linen, thick silk, and fine flannel. They colored the whole room. Suddenly, Daisy leaned down into the shirts and began crying loudly.

"These shirts are incredibly beautiful," she cried. "It makes me sad because I've never seen shirts this beautiful before."

108 After exploring the house, we planned to spend time in the swimming pool, and even the hydroplane.

"It's a little rainy. If it was not, we could see your home across the bay," Gatsby said. "You always have a green light that stays lit all night at the end of your dock."

Daisy suddenly linked her arm with his, but he seemed lost in his own thoughts. Maybe he realized that the enormous importance of that light had now disappeared forever. When he was so far away from Daisy, it felt like that light was so close to her, almost touching her. It seemed as near to her as a star to the moon. Now it was just a green light on a dock. One less magical thing in his world.

I started exploring the room, examining different objects in the dim light. There was a big picture hanging on the wall above his desk. It showed an older man dressed in yachting clothes.

"Who's this?" I asked.

"That? That's Mr. Dan Cody, old sport," Gatsby replied.

There was a small picture of Gatsby on the dresser. In the picture, he had his head thrown back, wearing the same yachting outfit. He looked about eighteen.

"I love it," Daisy exclaimed. "That hairstyle! You never told me you had that style—or a yacht."

109 "Look at this," Gatsby said quickly. "I have a lot of articles about you."

They stood next to each other, examining the cut out articles. Then the phone rang.

"Yes... I can't talk now... I can't talk now, old sport... I said a small town... He should know what a small town is... Well, he's not useful to us if he thinks Detroit is a small town..."

He hung up the phone.

Daisy and Gatsby looked up at the cloudy sky.

I tried to leave, but they didn't want me to.

"I have an idea," Gatsby said. "Let's have Klipspringer play the piano."

He left the room calling for "Ewing!" and came back a few

minutes later with a shy, tired-looking young man. He had glasses with thin frames and light blond hair. He was wearing a casual shirt, open at the neck, sneakers, and light-colored pants.

"Did we stop your nap?" Daisy asked politely.

"I was sleeping," Mr. Klipspringer said, shyly.

"Klipspringer plays the piano," Gatsby interrupted. "Right, Ewing?"

"I don't play well. I hardly play at all. I haven't practiced—"

We headed downstairs and Gatsby lit a cigarette for Daisy.

"Don't talk so much, my friend," commanded Gatsby. "Play!"

"In the morning, in the evening, ain't we got fun—"

Outside, the wind was loud, and there was distant thunder along the Sound. All the lights were turning on in West Egg now. The electric trains, carrying people, were rushing through the rain from New York. It was a time of big changes, and excitement filled the air.

"One thing's sure and nothing's surer, the rich get richer and the poor get—children. In the meantime, in between time—"

As I went to say goodbye, I noticed that Gatsby's face looked confused again. It was like he had a small doubt about how happy he really was. It had been almost five years and maybe there were times when he thought Daisy wasn't what he remembered. It wasn't her fault, it was just because his imagination was so big. It had become more than just about her, it was everything to him. He had put all of his passion into it. It's hard to beat the love a person keeps in their heart.

As I watched him, he adjusted himself a little. She whispered something to him. He turned to her with so much love. I think her voice held him the most, with its changing, passionate warmth. No dream could ever surpass it. Her voice was like a song that would never end.

I felt myself disappearing from their view. Then I left the room, walked down the marble steps in the rain, and left them there together.

SIX

112 AROUND THAT TIME, a young reporter from New York came to Gatsby's house one morning. He asked if Gatsby had something to say.

"What do you want me to talk about?" Gatsby asked politely.

It was a chance for the reporter, but his guess was correct. Gatsby had become well-known because many people had been to his parties and thought they knew about his past. During the summer, everyone knew his name. People started making up stories about him. It's hard to say why these made-up stories made James Gatz from North Dakota happy.

113 Once there was a young man named James Gatz. He didn't like his name, so he changed it to Jay Gatsby when he was seventeen years old. It was an important moment in his life when he saw a yacht called the Tuolomee on Lake Superior. Jay Gatsby was standing on the beach wearing old clothes, but he had big dreams. He took a rowboat and went out to the yacht. He told the owner, Dan Cody, that a storm might come and destroy the yacht in thirty minutes.

Maybe Gatsby had already planned to change his name. His parents were not successful farmers, and he never felt like he fit in with them. Gatsby believed he was special, like the son of God. He wanted to be involved in something important and beautiful. So, he created a new version of himself, the kind of person a seventeen-year-old would want to be. Gatsby stayed true to this vision until the end.

114 He lived and worked by Lake Superior, doing different jobs like digging clams and fishing for salmon to get food and a place to sleep. His body became tough and strong from the hard work. He met women at a young age although he often struggled to understand them.

But inside, his heart was constantly in pain. When he went to bed at night, strange and wild ideas filled his mind. His imagination created a world of bright and flashy things. These dreams helped him escape from reality. They showed him that the world could be like a magical place, where everything was perfect.

115 A feeling deep inside him told him that the future would be amazing. Acting on that feeling, he went to a small college called St. Olaf's in southern Minnesota. He didn't stay long though. He didn't have the patience. He also hated working as a janitor to pay for school. So, he returned to Lake Superior, still searching for something to do.

It was on that day that a wealthy man named Dan Cody's yacht anchored near the shore. Cody was fifty years old and had made his fortune in silver and gold. While he was physically strong, he was starting to lose his mental sharpness, and many women tried to take advantage of him for his money. He had been sailing along various shores for five years when he suddenly appeared as James Gatz's destiny in Little Girl Bay.

116 To young Gatz, as he rested on his oars and looked up at the deck, the yacht represented everything he wanted. Cody saw him and asked him a few questions, including one that resulted in Gatz receiving a brand new name. Cody discovered that Gatz was quick and had big dreams. A few days later, Cody took Gatz and bought

him a blue coat, six pairs of white pants, and a yachting hat. They sailed around and Gatsby went along.

He had a vague job title—while he was with Cody, he served as a steward, assistant, captain, secretary, and even a jailer. When Cody was sober, he knew that Gatsby had to keep a close eye on him to prevent any wild behavior. So, Cody trusted Gatsby more and more. This arrangement lasted for five years. Then, Cody unfortunately passed away.

117 I remember seeing a picture of him on the wall in Gatsby's room. He was a gray and flushed man with a tough, expressionless face. Because of Cody's influence, Gatsby didn't drink much.

Gatsby also received money from Cody after Cody died. Well, he was supposed to receive twenty-five thousand dollars. However, he never actually received it. He didn't understand the legal tricks that were used against him: the fees and such. The remaining millions ended up going to Ella Kaye, a woman with whom Cody had been involved. Everyone knew she was after Cody's money from the beginning. Still, Gatsby grew into a successful man.

Later on, he told me this story. The rumors about his life were completely false. He shared the truth with me when I began questioning him about his life.

118 For a few weeks, I didn't see him or hear his voice on the phone.

I visited his house one Sunday afternoon. I hadn't been there for even two minutes when someone brought Tom Buchanan in for a drink. I was surprised.

There were three of them on horses. Tom, a man called Sloane, and a pretty woman.

"I'm so glad to see you," said Gatsby, standing on his porch. "I'm happy that you stopped by."

As if they cared!

Tom's presence deeply affected Gatsby. However, he wanted to be polite and welcoming.

Gatsby turned to Tom, acted as if they were strangers.

"I think we've met somewhere before, Mr. Buchanan."

"Oh, yes," said Tom, "So we did. I remember very well."

"I know your wife," continued Gatsby, almost aggressively.

"We should all come to your next party, Mr. Gatsby," the woman suggested. "What do you say?"

"Of course, I'd be thrilled to have you."

"That would be very nice," said Mr. Sloane, without showing any thanks. "Well, we should be heading home."

"Please don't rush," Gatsby urged them. "Why don't you—why don't you stay for dinner? I wouldn't be surprised if more people from New York dropped by."

"Or you should join us for dinner," the lady said enthusiastically. "Both of you."

This included me. Mr. Sloane stood up.

"Come along," he said—but only to her.

"I mean it," she insisted. "I would love to have you. There's plenty of room."

Gatsby looked at me questioningly. He wanted to go, and he didn't understand that Mr. Sloane had decided he should not.

"I'm afraid I won't be able to," I said.

"Well, you should come," she urged, focusing on Gatsby.

Mr. Sloane murmured something close to her ear.

"We won't be late if we leave now," she insisted out loud.

"I don't have a horse," said Gatsby. "I used to ride in the army, but I never bought a horse. I'll have to follow you in my car. Sorry, just give me a minute."

The rest of us went outside on the porch. Sloane and the lady started talking excitedly to each other.

"Oh no, I think the man is coming too," said Tom. "Doesn't he know she doesn't want him?"

"She says she does want him."

"She's having a big dinner party and he won't know anyone there." He frowned. "I wonder where he met Daisy. I might be old-fashioned, but I don't like how much women run around these days. They meet all sorts of strange people."

Suddenly, Mr. Sloane and the lady walked down the steps and got on their horses.

"Come on," Mr. Sloane said to Tom. "We're late. We have to go." Then, he said to me, "Tell him we couldn't wait, okay?"

Tom and I shook hands, the others just nodded, and they quickly rode down the driveway and disappeared under the trees just as Gatsby, holding his hat and light coat, came out of the front door.

Tom seemed upset that Daisy was going out alone. The next Saturday he brought her to Gatsby's party. It was different from his other parties that summer. It felt uncomfortable and harsh.

They arrived at sunset.

"Take a look around," Gatsby suggested.

"I am looking around. It's amazing—"

"You must see the faces of many people you've heard about."

Tom proudly scanned the crowd.

"We don't go out much," he said. "Actually, I was just thinking that I don't know anyone here."

"Maybe you know that lady." Gatsby pointed to a beautiful woman. Tom and Daisy stared, feeling like they were seeing a famous ghost from the movies.

"She's lovely," said Daisy.

"The man next to her is her director."

Gatsby introduced them to different groups:

"Mrs. Buchanan... and Mr. Buchanan—" After a moment, he added, "the polo player."

"Oh no," Tom quickly objected, "not me."

But Gatsby liked the sound of it, so Tom was called "the polo player" for the rest of the evening.

"I've never met so many famous people," Daisy exclaimed. "I liked that man—what was his name?—with the blue nose."

Gatsby identified him as a small movie producer.

"Well, I liked him anyway."

"I'd rather not be known as the polo player," Tom said politely.

"I'd rather quietly observe all these famous people from the sidelines."

Daisy and Gatsby danced together. I was surprised by his graceful foxtrot—I had never seen him dance. Then they walked over to my house and sat on the steps for thirty minutes while I watched over the garden.

Tom interrupted our dinner. He asked, "Do you mind if I eat with those people? They seem to be having fun."

"Go ahead," Daisy responded cheerfully. I could sense that she was not enjoying herself.

We were sitting at a table with people who were rather annoying. I had sat with them only two weeks ago and enjoyed their company, but something was different.

Their conversation continued.

One of the last things I remember was standing with Daisy and watching a movie director and his lead actor. They were still standing together under the tree. He had been moving closer to her all night just to be this close. I saw him lean down one last time and kiss her cheek.

"I like her," Daisy said. "I think she's beautiful."

But everything else bothered her. She was horrified by West Egg and disturbed by its new energy that clashed with the old traditions.

I sat on the front steps with them while they waited for their car. It was dark and we could only see shadows.

"Who is this Gatsby anyway?" asked Tom suddenly. "I have a sense that his new money comes from working as an alcohol smuggler, you know."

"Not Gatsby," I replied shortly.

He stayed quiet for a moment. Tom laughed and turned to me. Daisy began to softly sing along to the music. She had a warm human magic that she put into the air.

"Well, I want to know who Gatsby is and what he does," Tom insisted. "And I'm going to find out."

"I can tell you right now," she replied. "He owned a bunch of drugstores. He worked hard to build them himself."

The slow limousine pulled up the driveway.

"Goodnight, Nick," Daisy said.

She glanced away from me and looked at the lit-up steps. In Gatsby's casual party, there were romantic possibilities that didn't exist in her world. What was it about that song that seemed to draw her back inside? What would happen now in the late hours? Maybe an incredible guest would arrive. Maybe an incredible young girl who would make Gatsby forget Daisy.

I stayed late that night. Gatsby asked me to wait until he was free. I stayed in the garden until the swimming party was over. Gatsby's face looked tight and his eyes were tired.

"She didn't enjoy it," he said right away. He fell silent, and I could tell he was very sad. "I feel distant from her," he said. "It's hard to make her understand." He wanted Daisy to do something important. He wanted her to go to Tom and tell him, "I never loved you." Once she said that, they could make plans for the future.

"And she doesn't understand," he said. "She used to understand. We would talk for hours—"

He stopped talking and started pacing on a lonely path with fruit peels and leftover decorations and crushed flowers.

"I don't think you should ask too much from her," I suggested. "You can't bring back the past."

"Can you bring back the past?" he asked in surprise. "Well, yes, you can!"

He looked around nervously, as if the past were hiding somewhere near his house, just out of his reach.

"I'm going to make everything exactly as it was before," he said firmly. "She'll see."

He talked a lot about the past. Maybe he was looking for something he had lost when he loved Daisy. His life had been messy and chaotic ever since, but maybe with her he could get back whatever was missing.

...One autumn night, five years ago, they were walking down the street as leaves were falling. They reached a place without trees, where the moonlight made the sidewalk look white. They stopped there and turned towards each other. It was a cool night with that special feeling that comes during the changing seasons. The quiet lights in the houses were shining into the darkness, and there was excitement in the air. Gatsby noticed, from the corner of his eye, that the sidewalk blocks formed a ladder that led to a secret place above the trees. He could climb it alone and once there, he could experience the magic of life, and feel the wonder all around him.

His heart raced as Daisy's face got closer to his. He knew that when he kissed her, his thoughts wouldn't be as wild and imaginative as before. He paused, listening to the sound in the air. Then, he kissed her. As their lips met, she seemed to come alive like a blossoming flower.

As he spoke, I couldn't help but feel a familiar rhythm, like a forgotten song I'd heard long ago. For a moment, I tried to say something but couldn't find the words. It felt like there was more than just air on my lips. But no sound came out, and I couldn't explain what I almost remembered.

CHAPTER
SEVEN

 IT WAS when people were most curious about Gatsby that the lights in his house didn't turn on one Saturday night. Just as mysteriously as it had started, his role finished. Worried that he might be sick, I went over to check on him. A butler answered the door.

"Is Mr. Gatsby sick?"

"Nope," he replied after a moment, reluctantly adding "sir."

"I haven't seen him around, and I was getting concerned. Let him know that Mr. Carraway came to visit."

The butler abruptly slammed the door shut.

My friend told me that Gatsby had fired all of his servants a week ago and hired a few others. People delivered things and said the house was a mess.

The next day, Gatsby called me on the telephone.

"Are you going somewhere?" I asked.

"No, old sport."

"I heard you fired of all your servants."

"I wanted someone who wouldn't spread rumors. Daisy comes over quite often--in the afternoons."

The whole inn had collapsed like a house of cards when Daisy disapproved.

"They're some people that Mr. Wolfshiem wanted to help. They're all brothers and sisters. They used to run a small hotel."

"I understand," I replied.

He called me because Daisy asked him to. She invited me to have lunch at her house tomorrow, and Miss Baker would be there too. Daisy sounded relieved when she learned that I would be coming. Something was going on. But I couldn't believe they would choose this occasion for a dramatic confrontation, especially the intense one Gatsby had described in the garden.

The next day was scorching hot, one of the warmest days of summer. On the train, a woman next to me was fanning herself and her purse dropped to the floor. I picked it up for her, but people looked at me oddly.

The conductor came by, said a few words, took my train ticket. He gave it back and it was damp with sweat from his hands.

A faint breeze blew through the hallway of the Buchanans' house. The butler approached us.

"Madam is waiting for you in the living room!" he exclaimed.

The room was cool and dim. Daisy and Jordan were lying on a big couch.

"We can't move," they said at the same time.

"And Mr. Thomas Buchanan, the athlete?" I asked.

At the same moment, I heard his gruff, muffled, and hoarse voice on the phone in the hallway.

Gatsby stood on the red carpet and looked around with curious eyes. Daisy watched him and giggled, her sweet, happy laugh.

"I heard a rumor," whispered Jordan, "that the person who keeps calling is Tom's girlfriend."

We didn't say anything. The voice in the hallway grew louder with frustration: "Fine, then! I won't sell you the car at all... I don't owe you anything... and I won't tolerate you bothering me about it during lunch!"

. . .

TOM BURST THROUGH THE DOOR, blocking it for a moment with his big body, and hurried into the room.

"Mr. Gatsby!" He reached out his wide, flat hand with hidden dislike. "I'm glad to see you, sir... Nick..."

"Make us a cold drink!" Daisy exclaimed.

As he left the room again, she got up and walked over to Gatsby, pulling his face down and kissing him on the mouth.

"You know I love you," she whispered.

"You forget there's a lady here," Jordan said.

Daisy looked around uncertainly.

"You should kiss Nick too."

"What a rude girl!"

"I don't care!" Daisy cried and began dancing on the brick fire-place. Then she remembered the heat and sat down guiltily on the couch.

"Hello, my darling," she sang, reaching out her arms. "Come to your mommy who loves you."

The child, let go by the nurse, quickly ran across the room and shyly hid in her mother's dress.

"Oh, my darling!'" Then Daisy directed her daughter to say hello to us.

Gatsby and I bent down and took the small hesitant hand in turn. Afterwards, he kept looking at the child with surprise. I don't think he had ever truly believed in her existence before.

"I got dressed before lunch," the child said eagerly, turning to Daisy.

"That's because mommy wanted to show you off." Daisy's face leaned close to the child's. "You're a dream, you know. You're an absolute little dream."

"Yes," the child calmly admitted. Daisy sat back on the couch. The nurse took a step forward and reached out her hand.

"Come, Pammy."

"Goodbye, sweetheart!"

The well-behaved child held onto her nurse's hand and was pulled out the door, just as Tom returned. He had four drinks with him. The ice clinked in the glasses.

Gatsby picked up his drink.

"They certainly look refreshing," he said.

We gulped down our drinks quickly.

"I learned that the sun is getting hotter each year," Tom said in a friendly tone. "Come outside," he suggested to Gatsby. "I want you to see the place."

I followed them outside to the porch. On the calm Sound, not moving in the heat, a small sailboat slowly made its way towards the cooler sea. Gatsby briefly watched it, then raised his hand and pointed across the bay.

"I'm right across from you."

"Yes, you are."

Our eyes looked beyond the rose gardens. We could see a boat's white wings moved slowly against the cool blue sky. Ahead, there were endless ocean waves and beautiful islands.

"That's something exciting," Tom remarked, nodding. "I wish I could be out there with him for an hour."

We had lunch in the dining room, which was also darkened to escape the heat. We drank cold ale to lighten the mood.

"What should we do this afternoon?" Daisy exclaimed. "Let's all go to town!"

Her voice fought against the heat, trying to give shape to the senselessness.

"I want to go to town!" Daisy said firmly. Gatsby looked at her and she exclaimed, "Wow, you look really cool."

Their eyes met, and they stared at each other, feeling like they were the only ones in the room. Daisy made an effort and looked down at the table.

"You always look so cool," she said again.

She had confessed her love to him, and Tom Buchanan noticed.

He was shocked. His mouth opened a bit, and he looked at Gatsby, then back at Daisy as if he recognized her from a long time ago.

"You look like the man in the advertisement," she innocently continued. "You know, the man in the advertisement..."

"Alright," Tom interrupted quickly, "I'm fine with going to town. Come on, we're all going to town."

He stood up, his eyes still flickering between Gatsby and his wife. Nobody moved.

"Let's go!" His temper began to crack. "What's the matter anyway? If we're going to town, let's start."

His hand, shaking from trying to control himself, brought the glass of ale to his lips for the last sip. Daisy's words made us all get up and go onto the scorching driveway.

"Let's have fun," she pleaded. "It's too hot to argue."

Tom didn't answer.

"Let's do what you want," she said. "Come on, Jordan."

"I don't understand why we're going to town," Tom said angrily. "Women get these ideas in their heads..."

"Should we bring something to drink?" Daisy called from an upstairs window.

"I'll get some whiskey," Tom answered. He went inside.

Gatsby turned to me, standing stiffly.

"I can't say anything in his house, old sport."

"She doesn't keep secrets well," I said.

"Her voice is full of money," he suddenly said.

That was it. I never understood it before. Her voice was full of money--that was the never-ending charm that came and went in it, the sound of coins clinking, the melody of it... Up high in a grand palace, the king's daughter, the golden girl...

Tom came out of the house, wrapping a bottle in a towel. Daisy and Jordan followed, wearing small hats made of shiny fabric and carrying light capes.

"Should we all go in my car?" Gatsby suggested. He touched the hot, green leather seat. "I should have parked it in the shade."

"Does the car have a manual transmission?" Tom asked.

"Yes."

"Well, here's an idea," said Tom. "You can take my car, and I'll drive your car to town."

Gatsby didn't like the suggestion.

"I don't think there's much gas left," he said.

"Don't worry, there's plenty of gas," said Tom loudly. He checked. "And if we run out, we can stop at a drugstore. You can buy anything at a drugstore nowadays."

Daisy looked at Tom with a frown.

"Come on, Daisy," said Tom, motioning for her to get into Gatsby's car. "I'll take you in this fancy car of his."

He opened the door, but Daisy stepped away from him.

"You go with Nick and Jordan. We'll follow you in the other car."

She walked close to Gatsby, touching his coat with her hand.

Tom looked and Jordan and me. He looked sharply, realizing that Jordan and I must have known about it all along.

"You must think I'm pretty dumb, huh?" he suggested. "Maybe I am, but sometimes I have a feeling. I have a feeling now."

"I looked into this guy a little," he said. "I could have found out more if I had known--"

"You mean you went to see a fortune teller?" Jordan asked jokingly.

"What?" Confused, he looked at us as we laughed.

"I saw a man who told me Gatsby's not an Oxford College graduate." He laughed, "Maybe Oxford, New Mexico, or something like that."

"Listen, Tom. If you're so stuck up, why did you invite him to lunch?" Jordan asked, annoyed.

"Daisy invited him. She knew him before we got married--who knows where!"

The hot weather made us all a little crazy. Then, when we saw Doctor T.J. Eckleburg's faded eyes on the road. I remembered Gatsby's warning about running out of gas.

"We have enough gas to get us to town," Tom said.

"But there's a gas station right here," Jordan objected. "I don't want to get stuck in this scorching heat."

Tom slammed on the brakes, and we came to a dusty stop under Wilson's sign. After a moment, the owner of the gas station came out and looked tiredly at the car.

"Let's have some gas!" Tom shouted. "We didn't stop to enjoy the view!"

"I'm not feeling well," said Wilson without moving. "I've been sick all day."

"Well, should I help myself?" Tom asked. "You sounded fine on the phone."

With effort, Wilson stepped out of the shade and let go of the door. Breathing hard, he unscrewed the gas tank cap. In the sunlight, his face looked pale.

"I didn't mean to interrupt your lunch," he said. "But I really need money, and I was wondering what you were planning to do with your old car."

"What do you think of this car?" Tom asked. "I bought it last week."

"It's a nice yellow one," said Wilson as he struggled with the handle.

"Interested in buying it?"

"Not really," Wilson weakly smiled. "But I could make some money with the other one."

"Why do you suddenly need money?"

"I've been here for too long. I want to go somewhere else. My wife and I want to go out West."

"Your wife does?" Tom exclaimed, surprised.

"She's been talking about it for ten years." He took a moment to rest against the pump, shading his eyes. "And now she's going, whether she wants to or not. I'm going to take her away."

The car sped by us, kicking up dust, and someone waved from inside.

"How much do I owe you?" Tom demanded, sounding harsh.

"I just found out something strange in the past two days," Wilson explained. "That's why I want to leave. That's why I've been bothering you about the car."

"How much do I owe you?"

"A dollar twenty."

141 The hot sun made me feel confused. I realized that Wilson hadn't suspected Tom of being with Myrtle just yet. He only knew that Myrtle had another life apart from him, and it made him sick. I looked at Wilson, then at Tom. It made me think that the biggest difference between people, no matter what, is the difference between being sick and being well. Wilson looked so sick that he seemed guilty, really guilty, like he had done something wrong to a girl.

"I'll give you that car," Tom said. "I'll send it to you tomorrow afternoon."

I felt uneasy. The giant eyes of Doctor T. J. Eckleburg watched over the ash-heaps. Then I realized that there were other eyes watching us intensely from just a short distance away.

142 As we looked up at the garage window, we saw the curtains being moved a little. Myrtle Wilson was peering down at the car. Then I understood that she wasn't looking at Tom, but at Jordan Baker, whom she thought was his wife.

～

THERE's no confusion like the confusion of a simple mind. Tom felt a wave of panic as we drove away. His wife and his girlfriend, who just an hour ago he thought he had control over, were slipping away from him. Tom hit the gas pedal, trying to catch up with Daisy and leave Wilson behind. We finally parked the car. Jordan said she felt excited to be in the city.

143 We saw Gatsby and Daisy. We realized we didn't know where to

go. Tom made a plan. "You follow me to the southern part of Central Park, in front of the Plaza Hotel."

As we drove, he looked back for their car, keeping an eye on them the whole time. I think he was scared that they might turn into a side street and disappear from his life forever.

But they didn't. And we all did something surprising by going into a fancy room in the Plaza Hotel.

It was still so hot. I remember feeling uncomfortable. My underwear was sticking to my legs and sweat dripping down my back.

The room was big and hot. Even though it was already four o'clock, opening the windows only let in hot air from the Park.

"This suite is nice," whispered Jordan, and everyone laughed.

"Open another window," Daisy said, without looking back.

"There aren't any more. The best thing to do is forget about the heat," Tom said, annoyed. "You're making it worse by complaining."

He took out the bottle of whiskey from the towel and put it on the table.

"Why don't you leave her alone, old sport?" Gatsby said. "You're the one who wanted to come to town."

There was a moment of silence.

"That phrase of yours is interesting," Tom said sharply.

"What phrase?"

"All this 'old sport' stuff. Where did you learn it?"

"Now wait a minute, Tom," Daisy said, turning away from the mirror. "If you're going to make personal comments, I won't stay here. Call and order some ice for the mint juleps."

As Tom picked up the phone, the stifling heat erupted into sound and we heard the important chords of Mendelssohn's Wedding March from the ballroom below.

"Imagine getting married in this heat!" Jordan exclaimed unhappily.

"I got married in the middle of June," Daisy remembered. "Louisville in June! Someone fainted. Tom will remember who."

The music stopped and the ceremony began. Then, people cheered and started dancing to lively jazz music.

"We're getting old," Daisy said. "If we were young, we'd dance too."

Tom and Jordan discussed the man who'd fainted at Tom and Daisy's wedding. His name was Bill Biloxi, and he had gone to Yale with Tom.

Gatsby's foot tapped nervously, catching Tom's attention.

"By the way, Mr. Gatsby, I heard you're an Oxford man."

"Not exactly," Gatsby replied.

"But I heard you went to Oxford," Tom continued.

"Yes, I did go there."

A pause. A waiter knocked and entered with crushed mint and ice, but the silence remained unbroken. Everyone wanted to know the truth.

"I told you I went there," Gatsby said.

"I heard you, but I want to know when," Tom questioned.

"It was in 1919, I only stayed for five months. That's why I can't really say I'm an Oxford man," Gatsby explained.

Tom looked at us, expecting us to be as shocked as he was. But we were all focused on Gatsby.

"They offered this opportunity to some officers after the war ended," he continued. "We could choose any university in England or France to attend."

I wanted to stand up and give Gatsby a pat on the back. He was so honest and calm.

Daisy stood up, smiling slightly, and went to the table.

"I have one more question for you Mr. Gatsby. What are you trying to do in my house?" Tom asked angrily.

"He's not causing any trouble," Daisy said. "You're the one causing trouble. Please, try to calm down."

"Calm down!" Tom repeated in disbelief. "I guess the new thing is to let some unknown person come and flirt with your spouse. Well, if that's what you want, count me out... Nowadays, people start by criticizing family life and traditions, and soon they'll throw every-thing away. Everything!"

Excited by his passionate words, he imagined himself standing alone on the last line of civilization.

"I know I'm not very popular. I don't throw big parties. I guess nowadays you have to make your house a mess to have any friends."

"Well, I have something to tell you, old sport..." started Gatsby. But Daisy understood what he was going to say.

"Please don't!" she shouted, feeling helpless. "Can we all just go home? Why don't we go home?"

"That's a good idea," I stood up. "Come on, Tom. Nobody wants a drink."

"I need to hear what Mr. Gatsby wants to tell me."

"Your wife doesn't love you," said Gatsby. "She's never loved you. She loves me."

"You must be crazy!" Tom responded.

Gatsby jumped to his feet excitedly.

"She never loved you, understand?" he shouted. "She only married you because I had no money and she couldn't wait for me. It was a big mistake, but deep down, she only loved me!"

I wanted to leave so badly and so did Jordan. Tom and Gatsby made us stay to watch the whole discussion.

"Please, Daisy, have a seat," Tom tried to sound comforting but failed. "Tell me everything that's been happening."

"I already told you what's been happening," Gatsby responded. "It's been happening for the past five years, and you didn't know."

Tom turned to Daisy with a sharp look.

"You've been seeing this man for five years?"

"I didn't say seeing," Gatsby explained. "No, we couldn't meet. But we loved each other."

"That's it? You're crazy!" he burst out. "I can't talk about what happened five years ago because I didn't know Daisy then. The things you've said are complete lies. Daisy loved me when she married me. She still loves me now."

"No," Gatsby shook his head.

"But she does! The problem is that sometimes she gets foolish thoughts in her mind and doesn't know what she's doing." Tom nodded wisely. "And you know what? I love Daisy too. Once in a while, I do something foolish, but I always come back, and deep in my heart, I love her all the time."

150 "You're disgusting," Daisy said. "Do you know why we left Chicago? I'm surprised no one told you about our little adventure."

Gatsby walked over and stood next to Daisy. He said, "It doesn't matter anymore. Just tell him the truth and that you never loved him. Then we can start fresh."

She hesitated. Her eyes pleaded with Jordan and me, as if she finally realized what she was doing. It was like she never meant to do anything at all. But it was too late. It had already happened.

"I never loved him," she admitted.

"Not even at Kapiolani?" Tom suddenly demanded.

"No."

From downstairs, we could hear muffled and heavy music filling the air.

"Not even on the day I carried you down from the Punch Bowl to keep your shoes dry?" His voice softened with tenderness. "Daisy?"

"Please stop," she said in a cold voice. She looked at Gatsby. "There, Jay," she said—though her hands shook.

151 "Oh, you expect too much!" she said to Gatsby. "I love you now, isn't that enough? I can't change the past." She started crying. "I used to love him, but I loved you too."

Gatsby blinked.

"Even that's not true," said Tom angrily. "She didn't know you were alive. There are things between Daisy and me that you'll never understand. We are husband and wife! I'll take better care of her."

"You don't understand," Gatsby panicked. "You won't take care of her anymore."

"I won't?" Tom laughed. "Why is that?"

"Daisy's leaving you."

"That's ridiculous."

"But I am," she said, struggling to say the words.

"She's not leaving me!" Tom's words hung over Gatsby. "Definitely not for a common cheat who had to steal the ring he put on her finger."

"I won't take this!" exclaimed Daisy. "Oh, please, let's leave."

"Who are you, anyway?" asked Tom. "You're one of those people who hangs out with Meyer Wolfshiem. You and Wolfshiem bought small drugstores here and in Chicago so you could sell alcohol. That's illegal."

"What's your point?" asked Gatsby politely. "I suppose your friend Walter Chase wasn't too ashamed to get involved."

"And you left him in trouble, didn't you? You let him go to jail for a month in New Jersey. Walter could expose you for breaking the betting laws too. But Wolfshiem scared him into keeping quiet."

That unfamiliar but familiar expression returned to Gatsby's face.

"That drugstore business was just a small thing," Tom continued slowly. "But now you're involved in something that Walter is afraid to tell me about."

I looked at Daisy, who was scared as she stared at Gatsby and her husband. Gatsby had a strange look on his face.

But that didn't last long, and he started talking excitedly to Daisy. He denied everything and defended himself against accusations that hadn't even been made. Daisy was slowly slipping away from him. Her bravery was gone.

"You two should go home, Daisy," Tom said. "You can ride in Mr. Gatsby's car."

Daisy looked at Tom, now alarmed.

"Go on. He won't bother you. I think he finally realizes that his silly flirting is over."

They left without saying a word. They seemed distant and separate, like ghosts, even though we felt sorry for them.

After a moment, Tom got up and started wrapping the unopened bottle of whiskey in a towel and offered us some.

I didn't say anything.

"Nick?" He asked again.

"What?"

"Do you want some?"

"No... I just remembered that today is my birthday."

I was turning thirty. In front of me was a long, scary road leading into a new decade.

It was seven o'clock when we got into the car with him and started driving to Long Island. I kept thinking about my life ahead. We kept driving as night fell and it became cooler.

There was a young Greek named Michaelis who worked at a coffee shop near the ash-heaps. He was the main person who gave information at the investigation. Michaelis had slept late because of the hot weather. When he finally woke up after five o'clock, he walked over to the garage and found George Wilson, his neighbor, in his office. Wilson looked really sick, as white as his own hair and shaking all over. Michaelis told him to go to bed, but Wilson didn't want to because he thought he would lose customers. While they were talking, they heard a loud noise coming from upstairs.

Wilson calmly explained, "I have my wife locked up there. She's going to stay there until the day after tomorrow, and then we're going to move away."

Michaelis was surprised. He had been Wilson's neighbor for four years, and Wilson had never seemed capable of saying something like that. Usually, Wilson was one of those tired men. When he wasn't working, he sat on a chair by the door and watched the people and cars passing by. Whenever someone talked to him, he would just laugh without much emotion. He was controlled by his wife and didn't make his own decisions.

Michaelis wanted to find out what happened, but George wouldn't say anything. Instead, he started looking at Michaelis strangely. Just when Michaelis started to feel worried, some workers came by. He was distracted by them. When he left the building again, he remembered the conversation because he heard Mrs. Wilson, George's wife, talking loudly and angrily downstairs in the garage.

A moment later, she ran out into the dark, waving her hands and shouting. Then, it was all over.

The "death car," as the newspapers called it, didn't stop. It came out of the dark and hesitated for a moment, then disappeared around the next turn. Michaelis wasn't even sure of the car's color, but he told the first policeman it was light green. The other car, the one going toward New York, stopped a hundred yards away, and the driver hurried back to Myrtle Wilson, who was now lifelessly kneeling on the road, her dark blood mixing with the dust.

157 Michaelis and another man arrived at her first. Her body was in bad shape.

WE SPOTTED the three or four cars and the crowd while we were still far away.

"Accident!" Tom said. "That's good. Wilson will finally have some business."

He slowed down. "We'll take a look," he said uncertainly, "just a quick look."

Now I noticed a hollow, mournful sound coming from the garage. It was a sound that turned into the words "Oh, my God!" repeated over and over in a gasping cry as we got out of the car and walked towards the door.

"There's some serious trouble here," Tom said.

He stood on tiptoes and looked over a group of heads into the garage. Then he made a harsh noise in his throat and forcefully pushed his way through with his strong arms.

158 The circle of people closed in.

Myrtle Wilson's body was covered with a blanket, and then

another blanket, as if she was cold on this hot night. It lay on a table against the wall. Tom was standing in front of it, not moving. There was a motorcycle policeman next to him, writing names in a small book. The policeman was sweating a lot and making corrections. He kept repeating his high, awful cry:

"Oh, my God! Oh, my God!"

Suddenly, Tom lifted his head and looked around with empty eyes. He told the policeman something.

"M-a-v—", the policeman started saying, "--o—"

"No, r—," corrected the man, "M-a-v-r-o—"

"Listen to me!" Tom interrupted fiercely.

"What happened? What happened?" Tom asked, confused.

"A car hit her. She died instantly. She ran out onto the road. The jerk didn't even stop his car."

"There were two cars," Michaelis said, trying to explain. "One coming, one going, you see?"

"Where were they going?" the policeman asked, interested.

"One going each way. Well, she"—his hand gestured towards the blankets but fell back down— "she ran out and the one coming from New York hit her, going thirty or forty miles an hour."

"What's the name of this place here?" the officer asked.

"It doesn't have a name."

A pale, well-dressed black man stepped forward.

"It was a yellow car," he said. "A big yellow car. Brand-new."

"Did you see the accident?" the policeman asked.

"No, but the car passed me on the road, going faster than forty. Maybe fifty, sixty."

"Come here and give me your name. Be careful. I need to get his name."

Some of this conversation must have reached Wilson, swaying in the office doorway, because suddenly a new topic emerged in his frantic cries:

"You don't have to tell me what kind of car it was! I know what kind of car it was!"

I observed Tom's back muscles tense under his coat. He quickly walked over to Wilson and, facing him, firmly grabbed his upper arms.

"You need to calm down," he said, trying to sound comforting.

Wilson saw Tom and tried to stand on his tiptoes, but he would have fallen if Tom hadn't kept him upright.

"Listen," Tom said, shaking Wilson gently. "I just arrived from New York a minute ago. I was bringing you that car we talked about. The yellow car I was driving this afternoon wasn't mine—do you understand? I haven't seen it all afternoon."

Only the African American man and I were close enough to hear Tom's words, but the policeman noticed something in his tone and looked at him suspiciously.

"What's going on?" the policeman asked.

"I'm his friend," Tom replied, turning his head but still holding Wilson steady. "He says he knows the car that caused the accident... It was a yellow car."

The policeman started to doubt Tom and asked, "What color is your car?"

"It's a blue car, a coupe," Tom answered.

"We just came from New York," I added.

Someone who was driving behind us confirmed this, and the policeman turned away.

"Now, if I could have that name again, please—"

Tom carried Wilson into the office like a doll, placing him in a chair. Then Tom closed the door behind them.

We lefr and pushed through the growing crowd.

Tom drove slowly until we turned the corner—then he suddenly accelerated. I heard a soft sob and saw tears streaming down his face.

"What a coward!" he whimpered. "He didn't even stop his car."

~

Suddenly, the Buchanan's house appeared in the distance.

"Daisy's home," he said. As we got out of the car, he glanced at me and frowned.

"I should have dropped you off in West Egg, Nick. There's nothing we can do tonight. I'll call a taxi for you to go home. Come inside."

"No, thanks. But please arrange for the taxi for me. I'll wait outside." I was feeling a bit ill and wanted to be alone. But Jordan stayed for a moment longer.

"It's only half-past nine," she said.

I refused to go inside. I had enough of everyone today, and that included Jordan too. She must have seen it in my face because she turned away quickly and hurried up the steps into the house. I sat down for a moment, holding my head in my hands. I waited at the end of the driveway for a taxi.

I hadn't gone far when I heard my name. Gatsby appeared from behind some bushes. By that time, I was feeling strange, and all I could think about was the brightness of his pink suit under the moonlight.

"What are you doing?" I asked.

"Just standing here, old sport."

Somehow, that seemed like a terrible thing to do. I wouldn't have been surprised if he was planning to rob the house any moment. I half expected to see scary faces, like the ones from "Wolfshiem's people," lurking in the dark bushes.

"Did you see any trouble on the road?" he asked after a minute.

"Yes."

He paused.

"Was she killed?"

"Yes."

"I figured as much. I told Daisy I thought so. It's better that the shock happens all at once. She handled it pretty well."

He spoke as if Daisy's reaction was the only thing that mattered.

"I took a back road to get to West Egg," he continued, "and

parked my car in the garage. I don't think anyone saw us, but I can't be certain."

I didn't like him very much at this point, so I didn't think it was necessary to tell him he was wrong.

"Who was the lady?" he asked.

"Her name was Wilson. Her husband owns the garage. How did it happen?"

"Well, I tried to turn the wheel—" He stopped talking, and suddenly I guessed the truth.

"Was Daisy driving?"

"Yes," he said after a moment, "but of course, I'll say I was. You see, when we left New York, she was very nervous, and she thought driving would calm her down—and this woman came running towards us just as we were passing another car. Everything happened so fast, but it seemed like she wanted to talk to us, like she thought we were someone she knew. Well, at first, Daisy turned away from the lady towards the other car, and then she got scared and turned back. As soon as I grabbed the wheel, I felt the impact—it must have killed her instantly. Anyway—Daisy stepped on the gas. I tried to make her stop, but she couldn't, so I pulled the emergency brake. Then she fell over into my lap, and I kept driving."

"She'll feel better tomorrow," he said. "I'm just going to stay here and see if he tries to bother her about what happened earlier. She locked herself in her room, and if he tries to be rough with her, she's going to turn the light off and on."

"He won't hurt her," I said. "He's not thinking about her."

"I don't trust him, my friend."

"How long will you wait?"

"All night, if I have to. At least until everyone goes to bed."

I had a new thought. What if Tom found out that Daisy was the one driving? He might think there's a connection. I looked at the house. There were a few bright windows downstairs and a pink light coming from Daisy's room on the first floor.

"You stay here," I said. "I'll check if there's any sign of trouble."

I looked inside the house through a window that was opened just slightly.

Daisy and Tom were sitting across rom each other at the kitchen table. The conversation was serious. Daisy nodded her head at what Tom said. They looked unhappy, but also cooperative with one another.

As I walked off the porch, I heard my taxi coming down the dark road towards the house. Gatsby was waiting for me where I had left him in the driveway.

"Is everything quiet up there?" he asked nervously.

"Yes, it's all quiet." I paused for a moment. "You should go home and get some sleep."

He shook his head.

"I want to stay here until Daisy goes to bed. Goodnight, my friend."

He put his hands in his coat pockets and turned back to watch the house. I walked away.

CHAPTER

EIGHT

 I COULDN'T SLEEP at all that night.

In the morning, I heard a taxi go up Gatsby's driveway. I raced out of bed to find him. I walked across his yard and noticed that his front door was still open. He was standing in the hallway looking sad.

"Nothing happened," he said sadly. "I waited. Around four o'clock she came to the window for a minute and then turned off the light."

"You should go away," I suggested. "They will find your car."

"Leave now, my friend?"

"Go to Atlantic City for a week or go up to Montreal."

 He didn't want to leave. He had to stay with Daisy until he knew what she would do. He was holding onto hope, and I couldn't bring myself to make him let go.

That night, he shared with me a strange story from his past with a man named Dan Cody. He shared it because his identity as "Jay Gatsby" had been shattered by Tom's mean words, and his big secret was now revealed. I think he would have confessed anything at that moment, but he wanted to talk about Daisy.

168 She was the first nice girl he had ever known. He had met people like her in the past, but there was always an invisible barrier between them. He found her very attractive. He went to her house for the first time, sometimes with other officers from Camp Taylor, and sometimes by himself. He was amazed--he had never been in such a beautiful house before. But the thing that made it so exciting was that Daisy lived there. To her, it was as casual as his tent at camp was to him. There was something intriguing about it, a hint of upstairs bedrooms that were more beautiful and cool than any other bedrooms. It felt like there were fun and joyful activities happening in every corner of the house. The romance was fresh and contemporary, not old and forgotten. It was filled with the scent of new motorcars and lively dances. It was also thrilling to know that many men had loved Daisy before him. It made her even more precious to him. He could sense their presence in the house, as if their emotions were still lingering in the air.

169 But he ended up in Daisy's house by a huge accident. Even though he might become a successful Jay Gatsby in the future, right now he was a poor young man with no past. At any moment, his uniform disguise could slip away. So he made the most of his time there. He took what he could, selfishly and dishonestly. Then one October night, he took Daisy, even though he had no real right to touch her hand.

He could have felt bad about himself because he had tricked Daisy. I don't mean that he used his fake wealth to win her over, but he made Daisy feel safe and secure. He let her believe that he was like her, from a similar background, and that he could take care of her. But in reality, he didn't have any of that.

But he didn't feel bad, and things didn't turn out the way he expected. He had planned to take what he could and leave, but now he found himself following Daisy. He knew Daisy was special, but he didn't realize just how remarkable a "nice" girl could be. She disappeared into her luxurious house, living a wealthy and fulfilling life, and left Gatsby with nothing. He felt like he was married to her, nothing more.

170   When they saw each other again, two days later, it was Gatsby who was breathless, who felt somehow let down. Her front porch was bright with the fancy shine of stars; the wicker of the sofa made a fashionable noise as she turned to face him. He kissed her mouth, which had a special curiosity and loveliness. She had caught a cold, making her voice hoarse and even more charming. Gatsby couldn't help but feel the power of youth and mystery that wealth creates.

"I can't really explain how surprised I was to realize I loved her, old sport. I even wished sometimes that she would break up with me, but she didn't because she loved me too. She thought I was knowledgeable because I knew different things than her... Well, there I was, far from achieving my dreams, falling deeper in love every minute, and suddenly I didn't care. What was the point of doing amazing things if I could have a better time just by telling her what I planned to do?"

171   On the day before he was going away, Gatsby sat with Daisy in his arms for a long time without saying anything. It was a cold day in the fall, and there was a fire in the room, making Daisy's cheeks red. They had never been closer than they were in that month of love, or understood each other so deeply.

Gatsby did exceptionally well in the war. Before he went to the front, he was a captain, and after the battles, he became a major and commanded the divisional machine-guns. When the war ended, he desperately tried to come home, but there were complications that sent him to Oxford instead. Daisy's letters showed that she was worried. She didn't understand why he couldn't come back. She felt the pressures of the outside world and wanted to see him.

Daisy was a young girl, living in a world that was full of fancy things. She was used to fancy flowers, orchestras, tea parties, and fresh faces.

As the season changed, Daisy started to enter this twilight world again. Suddenly, she was going on many dates again. Deep inside, she felt a need to make an important decision. She wanted her life to take shape right away.

In the middle of spring when Tom Buchanan arrived. He was big and important, and Daisy felt flattered by him. It was probably a bit difficult for her, but also a bit of a relief. Gatsby received the letter while he was still at Oxford.

~

THE SUN WAS RISING on Long Island, and we went downstairs to open the remaining windows, welcoming the house with soft gray and golden light.

"I don't think she ever loved him," Gatsby said, "He said things to her that scared her, making me seem like some kind of dishonest person. As a result, she hardly knew what she was saying."

He sat down sadly.

"Maybe she loved him for a moment when they first got married," he continued, "but she loved me even more back then, you see?"

He had come to realize something. I could see it in his eyes.

He came back from France when Tom and Daisy were still on their honeymoon. He made a sad but irresistible trip to Louisville, using the last of his army payment. He revisited special places he had been with Daisy.

He left with a feeling that if he had looked harder, he might have found her, but instead he was leaving her behind.

The train tracks curved and now they were heading away from

the setting sun, which seemed to bless the disappearing city where Daisy had lived. He reached out his hand desperately, as if trying to grab a small piece of the air, something to hold onto from the place that she had made beautiful for him. But everything was moving by too quickly for his blurry eyes, and he knew he had lost the freshest, best part of it forever.

At nine o'clock, after we had breakfast, we went on the porch. The weather had changed during the night and there was a fall feeling in the air. The gardener, the last servant of Gatsby, came to the bottom of the steps.

"I'm going to clean the pool today, Mr. Gatsby. Leaves will start falling soon, and then there's always trouble with the pipes."

"Don't do it today," Gatsby said. He turned to me with an apology. "You know, buddy, I haven't used that pool all summer?"

I looked at my watch and stood up.

"I have twelve minutes until my train."

I didn't want to go to the city. I wasn't worth working properly, but it was more than that—I didn't want to leave Gatsby. I missed that train, and then another one, before I could make myself leave.

"I'll call you," I finally said.

"Do that, buddy."

"I'll call you around noon."

We walked down the steps slowly.

"I guess Daisy will call too." He looked at me nervously, as if he wanted me to confirm this.

"I think so."

"Well, goodbye."

We shook hands and I started to leave. Just before I reached the hedge, I remembered something and turned around.

"They're a terrible crowd," I shouted across the lawn. "You're worth more than all of them combined."

I'm happy I said that. It's the only nice thing I ever said to him because I didn't approve of him. At first, he nodded politely, and then he smiled like we both knew this all along. His bright pink suit stood out against the white steps. I remembered the night I first came to his old home, three months ago. Everyone knew he was up to something bad, but he stood on those steps, hiding his dream that couldn't be spoiled, and waved them goodbye.

I thanked him for having me over. We always thanked him for that--me and the others.

"Goodbye," I called out. "I enjoyed breakfast, Gatsby."

BACK IN THE CITY, I tried to make a long list of stocks for a while, but then I fell asleep in my chair. Just before noon, the phone woke me up, and I jumped up with sweat on my forehead. It was Jordan Baker. She would often call me at this time because she was hard to find with all her moving around. Usually, her voice sounded fresh and cool, like a golf ball coming into the office window, but this morning it sounded harsh and dry.

"I've left Daisy's house," she said. "I'm in Hempstead now, and later today I'm going to Southampton."

It may have been polite to leave Daisy's house, but I felt annoyed by her actions. Her next comment made me tense.

"You weren't very nice to me last night."

"Why does it matter now?"

There was a moment of silence. Then:

"However, I want to see you."

"I want to see you too."

"What if I don't go to Southampton and come into town this afternoon?"

"No, I don't think this afternoon."

"Okay then."

"It's not possible this afternoon. There are various reasons--"

We talked like that for a while, and then suddenly we stopped talking. We hung up.

A few minutes later, I called Gatsby's house, but the line was busy. I tried four times. Finally, an annoyed operator told me they were keeping the line open for a long-distance call from Detroit.

~

178   I GOT on a train and tried to keep to myself. I didn't want to hear talk of Myrtle Wilson's death. Now I want to go back a little and tell you what happened at the garage after we left there the night before.

They had trouble finding Catherine, Myrtle's sister. She must have broken her rule against drinking. When she arrived, she was really drunk and couldn't understand that the ambulance had already left. She fainted. Someone, who was either kind or curious, took her in his car and followed the ambulance that was carrying her sister's body.

179   Late into the night, a crowd gathered in front of the garage while George Wilson sat on the couch inside. He rocked himself back and forth. Michaelis stayed with Wilson until the sun came up.

Around three o'clock in the morning, Wilson became quieter and started talking about a yellow car. He said that he had a way to figure out who the yellow car belonged to. Then he said a few months before, his wife had come from the city with bruises on her face and a swollen nose.

But as soon as he heard himself say this, he started crying "Oh, my God!" Michaelis tried to distract him.

"How long have you been married, George? Come on, try to sit still for a moment and answer my question. How long have you been married?"

"Twelve years."

"Did you ever have any children? Come on, George, stay still—I asked you a question. Did you ever have any children?"

180   Michaelis tried hard to distract him with questions, but Wilson fell silent. His eyes expressed confusion.

"Look in the drawer there," he said, pointing at the desk.

"Which drawer?"

"That one--that one."

Michaelis opened the closest drawer within reach. There was nothing inside except for a small, expensive dog leash made of leather and silver braids. It seemed brand new.

"This?" he asked, holding it up.

Wilson stared and nodded.

"I found it yesterday afternoon. My wife tried to tell me about it, but I knew there was something strange."

"Did your wife buy it?"

"She had it wrapped in paper on her dresser."

Michaelis didn't find anything strange about that, and he gave Wilson several reasons why his wife might have bought the dog leash. But it seemed like Wilson had heard similar excuses.

"Then he killed her," Wilson said, his mouth dropping open suddenly.

"Who did?"

"I have a way of finding out. He murdered her."

"It was an accident, George."

Wilson shook his head. His eyes squinted.

"I know," he said firmly. "I'm a trusting person, and I don't suspect anyone of harm. But when I know something, I know it. It was the man in that car. She ran out to talk to him, and he wouldn't stop."

Michaelis had also witnessed this, but it hadn't crossed his mind that there was anything significant about it. He believed that Mrs. Wilson had been running away from her husband, rather than trying to stop a specific car.

"How could she be like that?"

"She's secretive," Wilson said, as if that explained everything. "Ah-h-h—"

He started rocking again, and Michaelis stood holding the leash tightly.

"Maybe you have a friend that I can call for you, George?"

Michaelis knew it was unlikely that Wilson had any friends.

Wilson's eyes stared out at the ash heaps."I spoke to her," he mumbled, after a long quiet. "I told her she could trick me, but she couldn't trick God. You may fool me, but you can't fool God!'"

Standing behind him, Michaelis was shocked to see that Wilson was looking at the eyes of Dr. T.J. Eckleburg. They had just appeared in the morning sunlight, pale and huge.

"God sees everything," Wilson repeated.

"That's just an advertisement," Michaelis tried to tell him.

183 BY SIX O'CLOCK, Michaelis was tired and thankful to hear a car stop outside. It was one of the people who had been watching the night before. He had promised to come back. Michaelis made breakfast for three people, and he and the other man ate together. Wilson was quieter now, so Michaelis went home to sleep. When he went back to the garage, Wilson was gone.

They later found out that Wilson had been walking the whole time. Some boys saw him acting strangely, and some drivers noticed him staring at them. Then, he disappeared for three hours. The police believed that during that time, he went from one garage to another, asking about a yellow car. No garage worker ever confirmed who had one. Later on in the day, he was asking where Gatsby lived.

184 At two o'clock, Gatsby changed into his bathing suit and told the butler that if anyone called, they should tell him at the pool. He stopped by the garage to get a pool float that his guests enjoyed using during the summer. With the help of the chauffeur, he pumped it up. Then, he gave strict instructions that the car should not be taken out for any reason, even though the right front fender needed to be fixed.

Gatsby carried the float on his shoulder and headed towards the pool.

No phone message came. I think Gatsby himself didn't believe the message would come. He looked up at the sky while a ghostly figure approached him through the shapeless trees.

185 The driver heard the sounds of the shots. Later, he said he didn't think much about them at the time. I went straight to Gatsby's house from the train station. I rushed up the front steps in a worried hurry. The driver, the butler, the gardener and I had a bad feeling.

We rushed down to the pool. The pool float moved in a wobbly way, creating gentle ripples. A group of leaves caused it to rotate slowly, leaving a thin red circle in the water.

It was while we were walking back to the house with Gatsby's body that the gardener spotted Wilson's body in the grass nearby, and the chaos was complete.

CHAPTER

NINE

186 AFTER TWO YEARS I can only remember bits and pieces of what happened that day. After that, it felt like a never-ending parade of police officers, photographers, and reporters going in and out of Gatsby's front door. Little boys snuck in to see Gatsby's body even though the front gate to the driveway was locked. Wilson was described by the police and papers as a madman.

187 Most of the news stories were like a scary dream. They were weird, detailed, enthusiastic, and not true. When Michaelis spoke at the inquest and revealed Wilson's suspicions about his wife, I thought people would start making funny jokes. But Catherine, who could have said anything, didn't say a single word. She showed a surprising amount of strength--looked right at the person in charge, with determination in her eyes and her brows fixed, and swore that her sister never met Gatsby, that her sister was completely happy with her husband, and that her sister didn't do anything wrong. She convinced herself of this and cried into her handkerchief, as if the very idea was too much for her to bear. So they made Wilson out to be a grieving man who was "crazy" in order to keep the case simple. And that's how it ended.

But all of that seemed far away and not that important. I found myself on Gatsby's side, all by myself. Everyone looked to me for answers, which was surprising to me at first.

I called Daisy about thirty minutes after we found him. I called her right away and without hesitation. But she and Tom had gone away earlier that day and took their things with them.

"Do you know where they went? Do you know when they'll be back?"

"No."

"Do you have any idea where they are or how I can reach them?"

"I don't know. I can't say."

I wanted to find someone for Gatsby. I wanted to go into the room where he was and reassure him: "I'll find someone for you, Gatsby. Don't worry. Just trust me and I'll find someone for you."

I couldn't find Meyer Wolfshiem's name in the phone book. The butler told me his office was on Broadway, so I called Information. But by the time I got the number, it was already late, and no one answered the phone.

I was alone and I imagined Gatsby telling me that he, too, was alone.

I hurriedly went upstairs and searched through the open parts of his desk. He never told me for sure if his parents were dead. But there was nothing there except for a picture of Dan Cody hanging on the wall.

The next morning, I sent the butler to New York with a letter for Wolfshiem. I asked for information and urged him to come on the next train. At the time, it felt unnecessary because I was certain he would be startled when he saw the newspapers, just as I was certain Daisy would send a message before noon. But neither a message nor Mr. Wolfshiem arrived. Only more police, photographers, and reporters showed up. When the butler returned with Wolfshiem's response, I started feeling annoyed, like Gatsby and I were united against them all.

Dear Mr. Carraway,

This has been a shock to me, one of the worst in my life. It's hard to believe it's true. What that man did was insane and it makes us all think. I can't come down right now as I'm caught up in very important business and can't be involved in this situation. If there's anything I can do later, let me know in a letter through Edgar. I'm so unsettled when I hear about something like this; it really knocks me down.

Yours truly,

Meyer Wolfshiem

P.S. Let me know about the funeral and all. I don't know his family at all.

When the phone rang that day, and Long Distance said Chicago was calling, I hoped it was Daisy. But instead, it was a man named Slagle.

"Hello," I said, not recognizing the name.

"Bad news, huh? Did you get my message?" he asked quickly.

"No, I haven't received any messages," I replied.

"Trouble with young Parke. They caught him trying to sell some bonds. The police got a notice from New York with the bond numbers just five minutes before. Can you believe it? You can't trust anyone in small towns like this."

"Wait!" I interrupted, out of breath. "This isn't Mr. Gatsby. Mr. Gatsby has passed away."

There was a long silence on the other end. Then, I heard an exclamation, followed by a sudden ending to the call.

I THINK it was three days later when a telegram arrived from a place called Minnesota. It was signed by Henry C. Gatz. The message said that he was coming right away and asked to postpone the funeral until he arrived.

It was Gatsby's dad, an old man who looked sad, weak, and

worried. He was wearing a long, cheap coat even though it was warm in September. He was tearful and barely able to stand.

"I read about it in the newspaper from Chicago," he said. "It was all in the newspaper. I came right away."

"I didn't know how to contact you."

His eyes were moving around the room, even though he couldn't see anything.

"He was crazy," he said. "He must have been crazy."

"Do you want some coffee?" I asked him.

"I don't want anything. I'm fine now, Mr.—"

"Carraway."

"Well, I'm fine now. Where is Jimmy?"

I took him to the room where his son was lying and left him there. Some boys were standing at the entrance, looking inside. When I told them who had arrived, they left slowly.

After a little while, Mr. Gatz opened the door and came out. His face was red and he had tears in his eyes.He felt sad but also proud. I helped him to a bedroom upstairs. As he took off his coat, I told him that everything had been put on hold until his arrival.

"I didn't know what you would want, Mr. Gatsby—"

"Gatz is my name."

"—Mr. Gatz. I thought you might want to take the body out West."

He shook his head.

"Jimmy always liked the East better. He became successful in the East. Were you a friend of my son's, Mr.—?"

"We were close friends."

"He had a bright future ahead of him, you know. He was young but very smart."

He pointed to his head, and I nodded. After that, he slept in one of the bedrooms for a long time.

That night, someone called and sounded scared. They wanted to know who I was before giving their name.

"This is Mr. Carraway," I said.

"Oh!" They sounded relieved. "This is Klipspringer, the pianist."

193 I was happy to hear Klipspringer's voice on the phone because it meant there might be another person at Gatsby's funeral. I didn't want strangers showing up because they read about it in the newspapers. So, I had been calling a few people myself, but it was hard to reach them.

"The funeral is tomorrow," I said. "At three o'clock, here at the house. I hope you can tell anyone who might be interested."

"Oh, I will," he said quickly. "I may not see anyone, but if I do."

His words made me suspicious.

"But you'll be there, right?"

"Well, I'll definitely try. Actually, the truth is I'm staying with some friends in Greenwich, and they expect me to be with them tomorrow. They're having a picnic or something. But I'll do my best to leave and come."

I couldn't help but mutter, "Huh!" He must have heard me because he continued nervously:

"The reason I called was because I left a pair of shoes there. I was wondering if it would be too much trouble for the butler to send them to me. You see, they're my tennis shoes, and I feel lost without them—"

I hung up the phone.

194 I felt a bit guilty for Gatsby after that. One person I called seemed to think he deserved what happened to him.

On the day of the funeral, I went to New York to find Meyer Wolfshiem. I couldn't reach him any other way. A woman answered his office door.

Then I heard Wolfshiem's voice calling "Stella!"

"I'll leave your name and a message," she quickly responded.

"But I know he's in there."

She took a step towards me and looked very angry.

195 "You young folks think you can just barge in here whenever you want," she scolded. "We're tired of it. When I say he's in Chicago, he's in Chicago."

I mentioned Gatsby.

"Oh-h!" She looked at me again. "What was your name?"

Then she disappeared. Soon after, Meyer Wolfshiem came through the doorway, extending both hands. He pulled me into his office and offered me a cigar.

"I remember when I first met him," he said. "I pulled him up from nothing, right from the streets. I saw right away that he was a well-mannered and well-dressed young man, and when he told me he attended a prestigious school, Oxford, I knew he would be useful. I got him to join the American Legion, and he made quite a name for himself there. Soon, he did work for a client of mine in Albany. We were inseparable, always together," he said, holding up his two plump fingers.

I wondered if they had done business together during the World's Series in 1919.

"Now he's gone," I said after a moment. "Since you were his best friend, I know you'll want to come to his funeral this afternoon."

"I can't do it—I don't want to be involved," he said.

"There's nothing to be involved in. It's all over now."

"When someone gets killed, I prefer not to be a part of it in any way. I stay out of it. When I was younger, it was different—I would stick by my friends until the end, no matter how. You might think that's emotional, but I mean it—to the very end."

I realized that he had his own reasons for not wanting to come, so I stood up. When I left his office, the sky had turned dark and I returned to West Egg in a light rain. After changing my clothes, I went to the neighboring house and found Mr. Gatz pacing in the hallway. His pride in his son was growing. He wanted to show me something.

"Jimmy gave me this picture." He took out his wallet with shaky hands. "Look here."

It was a photo of the house, cracked and dirty. He eagerly pointed out every detail to me. "Look here! He came to visit me two years ago and bought me the house I live in now. We had some disagreements when he ran away from home, but now I understand why he did it. He knew he had a bright future ahead. And ever since he became successful, he has been very kind to me."

He seemed hesitant to put away the picture, holding it in front of my eyes for another minute. Then he put the photo back in his wallet and took out a worn-out book called Hopalong Cassidy.

"Look here, this is a book he had when he was a boy. It just shows you."

He opened it to the back cover and turned it for me to see. On the last page, it said "schedule" and the date September 12, 1906. And underneath:

Wake up — 6:00 am

Exercise and climb walls — 6:15–6:30

Study electricity, and more — 7:15–8:15

Work — 8:30–4:30

Play baseball and sports — 4:30–5:00

Practice speaking and poise — 5:00–6:00

Study important inventions — 7:00–9:00

General Plans

"I found this book by accident," the old man said. "It really shows something, doesn't it?"

"It sure does."

"Jimmy always had goals."

He didn't want to close the book, reading each thing out loud and looking at me excitedly. I think he expected me to copy the list for myself.

A little before three, the preacher from the Lutheran church came to the house.. As time went by and the servants came in and waited in the hallway, Mr. Gatz's eyes started to blink nervously, and he mentioned the rain in a worried way. The preacher looked at his watch a few times, so I spoke to him privately and asked him to wait for another thirty minutes. But it didn't matter. No one came.

❧

199 AROUND FIVE O'CLOCK, our group of three cars arrived at the cemetery and stopped by the gate in a heavy drizzle. Mr. Gatz and the preacher arrived first. A little later, a few wet servants and the mailman from West Egg arrived. I saw the man with owl-shaped glasses who I had seen marveling at Gatsby's books in the library a few months ago.

After a short ceremony, we hurried back to the cars through the rain. By the gate, the man with owl-shaped glasses spoke to me.

"I couldn't get to the house," he said.

"Nobody could," I replied.

"Unbelievable! After all the people who came to his parties?" He took off his glasses and wiped them once more, on the outside and on the inside.

200 "The poor man," he said.

~

I HAVE a strong memory of coming back home from boarding school during Christmas time. After finishing high school and later college, I would return to the West. At six o'clock on a December evening, those who traveled beyond Chicago would gather at the old Union Station. I can still picture the girls wearing fur coats, returning from their fancy schools, and the sound of their breath freezing in the air as they chatted. They talked about this person and that.

When the train pulled out into the winter night and we were surrounded by real snow, our snow, we could see it twinkling against the windows. As we passed small stations in Wisconsin, the dim lights of those places moved by. We could feel connected to the countryside and others, before melting away again.

201 That's my Midwest. It's the exciting trains coming back from my childhood. I belong to that world. I feel proud having grown up in the Carraway house in a city where houses are still known by a family's name over many years. Now I realize that this has been a story of the West all along. Tom and Gatsby, Daisy and Jordan, and I, all

being from the Midwest. Maybe we all had something in common that made us not quite fit into Eastern life.

202   Even when I was most excited about the East, even when I knew it was better than the boring towns near where I was from, it always seemed strange to me. West Egg, in particular, appears in my wildest dreams. It glittering, but also sad and careless.

After Gatsby died, the East haunted me in that same distorted way, beyond what my eyes could correct. So, when the air was filled with the scent of crisp leaves, I decided to return home.

There was one thing I had to do before I left. I met with Jordan Baker and talked about what had happened to us and what had happened to me afterwards. She listened.

203   She was wearing clothes for playing golf, and I thought she looked like an illustration, with her chin held up in a little jazzy way, her hair the color of a leaf in the fall. Her face was the same light brown shade as the glove on her knee. When I finished talking, she told me without saying anything that she was engaged to another man. I didn't believe that, even though there were many men she could have married with just a nod.

She said that I had broken up with her. I wondered if I had made a mistake. We shook hands.

"Oh, and do you remember," she added, "a talk we had once about driving a car?"

"Well, not exactly."

"You said a bad driver is only safe until she meets another bad driver? Well, I met another bad driver, didn't I? I mean, I was careless to make such a wrong guess. I thought you were an honest, straight-forward person. I thought that was something you valued."

"I'm thirty," I said. "I'm five years too old to lie to myself and call it honor."

She didn't say anything. Angry, half in love with her, and very sorry, I turned away.

~

204   ONE AFTERNOON IN LATE OCTOBER, I saw Tom Buchanan. He was walking ahead of me on Fifth Avenue, moving quickly with his hands slightly out from his body like he was ready to defend himself. His head was moving in different directions, always looking around with restless eyes. Just as I slowed down to avoid passing him, he suddenly stopped and started to stare into the windows of a jewelry store. Then, he spotted me and walked back toward me, extending his hand.

"What's wrong, Nick? Do you have a problem shaking hands with me?"

"Yes. You know what I think of you."

"You're wrong, Nick," he said hurriedly. "You're completely wrong. I don't understand why you feel this way."

"Tom," I asked, "what did you say to Wilson that day?"

He looked at me without saying a word, and I knew I had guessed correctly about those missing hours. I began to turn away, but he took a step towards me and grabbed my arm.

"I told him the truth," he said. "He came to the door when we were getting ready to leave, and when I told him we weren't there, he tried to come inside forcefully. He was desperate enough to harm me if I didn't tell him who owned the car. He had a gun in his pocket the whole time he was at the house..." He paused, standing firm. "So what if I told him? He deserved it. Just like he deceived you and Daisy, he was a violent man. He ran over Myrtle like he would run over an animal and didn't even stop his car."

205   There was nothing I could say, except for the one thing that wasn't true.

"And if you think I didn't have my fair share of suffering—look here, when I went to give up that apartment and saw that darn box of dog treats on the table, I sat down and cried like a baby. It was terrible—"

I couldn't forgive him or like him, but I realized that, to him, what he did made sense. It was all very careless and confusing. Tom and Daisy were careless people—they broke things and hurt living beings, then hid behind their money, and let someone else clean up the mess they caused...

I shook his hand. It felt silly not to, because in that moment, I felt like I was talking to a child. The whole thing made me let go of disliking small-town living forever.

~

GATSBY'S HOUSE was still empty when I left.

On Saturday nights, I would spend my time in New York because Gatsby's amazing parties were still fresh in my mind. I could still hear the music and laughter coming from the garden, and see the cars going up and down his driveway. One night, I heard a car pull up and stop at his front steps, but I didn't investigate. It was probably just a late guest who didn't realize the party was over.

On the final night, after packing my belongings and selling my car to the grocer, I went to Gatsby's house one last time. The house was huge and messy, a failure in many ways. On the bright white steps, someone had written a rude word with a piece of brick. I erased it, scraping my shoe against the stone. Then, I walked down to the beach and laid down on the sand.

Most of the big beach places were closed now and there were hardly any lights except for a faint, moving glow from a boat across the water.

I sat there thinking about the old, unknown world. I remembered how Gatsby must have felt when he saw the green light at the end of Daisy's dock. His dream must have seemed so close. He didn't know that it was already in the past.

Gatsby believed in the green light, in a future that always seems far away. We couldn't catch it then, but that doesn't matter—we'll try harder tomorrow, reach out even further... And one fine morning—

So we keep going, like boats pushed against the water, yet always pulled back to the past.